THROWN TO THE WOLVES
THE LEGEND OF HANNAH & ELI

VERONICA BLADE

PUBLISHING

Gardnerville, Nevada

THROWN TO THE WOLVES

Crush Publishing, Inc
Gardnerville, NV 89460
www.CrushPublishing.com

Crush Publishing, Inc name and logo are trademarks of Crush Publishing, Inc and are used only with its permission.

The places, characters and events portrayed in this book are fictitious. Any similarity to real persons, living or dead, is coincidental and not intended by author.

ISBN 978-0-9910756-3-8

Cover design and layout by Rose Nomura

Printed in the United States of America

THROWN TO THE WOLVES
THE LEGEND OF HANNAH & ELI

EXCERPT

I NEEDED TO make this excursion to the forest count.

After a check to make sure no guards lurked nearby, I jumped from the smithy window and raced toward the trees, moving faster than I ever had in my life. Once under the cover of the forest, I stood absolutely still and listened for any werewolves who might have followed me. There were none.

But something else was out there. I could sense its energy.

I spun, my heart pounding against my ribs, my stomach fluttering at the sight of the beautiful blond blacksmith standing a yard away.

His eyes narrowed as his gaze swept over me. "The bow, quiver and arrows... I believe they belong to me."

My mouth dropped open. Why had I not been aware he was following me? A scent drifted to me, but I could not place it. Sweet with a hint of earth.

"I saw you leave the smithy." He nodded toward the quiver slung over my shoulder. "My father made those for me when I was twelve and the arrows were carved by my hand. I would be most grateful if you would return them, milady."

I glanced at the bow and quiver, unwilling to give them up. I needed them. "I regret I am unable to relinquish them, sir, but I shall be happy to compensate you for your trouble."

His stance remained respectful with his head bowed, but his words were clipped. "My father's gifts are not for sale."

Letting the weapons go was not an option, though. As a werewolf, especially a born one, I had the advantage of strength against shape-shifters. Still, I did not want to take any chances. I raised my chin and angled my shoulder so he could not easily snatch the bow. "I shall do everything in my power to return your belongings once I have no use for them. I am afraid, sir, that is my only offer."

FOR MEGAN & SHELBY

I really LOVE you guys.

CHAPTER ONE

Dover, England, 1358

I ENDURED A tedious supper with the man whom I was to marry, yet whose company I barely tolerated—and only because I had to. When expected, I smiled and when appropriate, I laughed. But I wanted to be anywhere else.

After everyone finally finished eating and a respectable amount of time passed, I begged my future husband—and sovereign—to be excused. After all, I had only just arrived after a two-day fifty-mile trip and needed to settle in. More urgently, over twenty-four hours had passed since I had last morphed into a wolf, and the need to shift pulsed through my veins like molten metal.

I hurried outside and practically stumbled in my haste. A few others had already arrived at the bailey—though I would have preferred the woods—and shifted into wolves, while a couple guards stayed in their human form to keep watch. Not that our kind were in danger of losing all good sense in our animal form, but emotions might be dulled or amplified, depending on the situation. In our wolf form, we were not as picky about food and may not mind eating it raw. Or our emotions could be amplified, making us prone to fighting. Fortunately, werewolves healed quickly.

Averting my eyes, I hoped no one would attempt to engage me in conversation. Since I did not intend to stay at the castle, I did not want anyone to form an attachment to me. And that included the blond shape-shifter I had glimpsed when I first arrived — no matter how drawn I was to him.

Always on alert, now that I was in unfamiliar surroundings, I glanced around the bailey. I had passed it that morning on the way to my chamber when I had first seen the blond shifter. At the time, handmaidens had surrounded me and the guards had swept me down the cobblestone path past the gate before I could take it all in.

Just like earlier, the stables sat to my right, and beyond that was the blacksmith's workshop where the blond man had been standing out front, his arms flexing as he wielded hammer against metal. He was tall and his muscles bunched beneath the plain white, billowy shirt.

All supernaturals emitted an energy, to a greater or lesser degree, which others could sense. As soon as I had gotten close enough, I knew he was not a werewolf.

Even if I had not sensed him, I would have known he was not human either, since the king had rules which forbade werewolves to involve mortals in anything more than trade or the occasional, obligatory hosting of royalty. The only way a shape-shifter could get into the castle was as a prisoner or slave.

He and I had common ground—we were both there against our will.

I had never met a shape-shifter, but had heard stories of the centuries-long war between our two species. I wondered what the blacksmith had done to seal his fate. Not that I would ever find out since it would not do for the king's betrothed to inquire about a slave, much less associate with one.

Yet when I had seen him, I could not help but watch him, the breadth of his shoulders and the strength in his arms as he let the hammer fall. He used a tong to flip over the red-hot slash of metal, then the hammer had crashed down again and I continued forward, though my eyes had remained on him. To avoid drawing attention to myself, I needed to avert my eyes. But I could not.

Glancing over his shoulder, he had caught my gaze and held it with his own deep blue eyes. For an instant, only he and I existed as I took in every inch of his beautiful face. Straight, blond hair fell over his forehead and brushed his prominent cheekbones. His jaw was strong, but not so angled that it showed evidence of age. He could not have been more than three or four years older than I.

He returned his attention to the block in front of him, and the spell was broken. I forced myself to look straight ahead, as metal against metal sounded once again.

Moments later, I had been guided into the castle.

Since I belonged to the king, I had no business looking at other men anyway.

Not that I truly belonged to the king either. Both the blacksmith slave and my betrothed would soon be a distant memory once I fled. Hopefully, I would not see the shape-shifter again since I could not afford the distraction. I would learn where the guards were posted, their routines and the layout of the castle. Somehow, I would store dried food in my chamber for my journey and find weapons for protection. Then, before the wedding in one month's time, I would flee.

But for now, I would act as if I were one of them. Every evening, I would morph in the bailey with the rest of the werewolves, then return to my chamber and dream of being free.

At a safe distance from the others, I sucked in a deep breath and relaxed my muscles. A small tremor began in my middle and traveled to my limbs. For just a moment, I felt weightless and an instant later, I stood on all fours.

I took off running as fast as I could, doing laps along the surrounding walls. After a few rounds, I cut my run short. I generally preferred solitude over the company of werewolves, who could be a fierce and foul-tempered lot. The objects of my disdain did not need to know my feelings, though. So when I shifted back to human again, I smiled at a couple who cast me a curious glance. I smoothed over my gown that had shifted with me, then left.

Up in my room, the finest tapestries lined the walls, with more space than I could possibly want. Yet as I lay in the enormous, four-poster bed over silk linens, one thought rang through my head: how would I escape?

I moved to my writing desk and wrote a letter to my mother, telling her about the handsome king who dazzled me with his charm. I prattled on about the castle's exquisite tapestries and the honor I felt each time a servant bowed before me. A few lines of gratitude to her for promising me to the werewolf king made my letter more convincing.

All lies, of course. I had to maintain an air of loyalty. I had been raised on stories of the werewolf king and his penchant for killing anyone who dared defy him. I knew that in order to revolt against him and succeed, I had to make certain no one knew what I was preparing to do. Everyone had to be convinced that their future queen was the most faithful of them all.

I doubted my tutor, Mrs. Benton, could be fooled. She had been my companion since my parents promised me to the king four years ago at age thirteen. Because my parents had never paid proper attention to me — my father always too busy leading the pack and my mother enjoying her new werewolf life — Mrs. Benton had been my lifeline. She knew me better than anyone and, in turn, I had learned to trust her more than my own family.

Where was she? I craved the comfort only she could provide. Lord knew I needed a distraction or my thoughts might go in unwanted directions—specifically to a blond shape-shifter.

A tap sounded at the door. "It is Mrs. Benton, milady."

Grinning, I sprung from the bed and flung open the door. "I am so pleased you came. I missed you in the great hall."

"And I, you. But I had business to attend to." Mrs. Benton returned my smile as she crossed the threshold, then held out a deck. "I brought cards to pass the evening. Would you like to play?"

"Very much. I shall ring for tea." I closed the door after her and motioned her to the settee. After shaking the bell, I pulled an end table toward Mrs. Benton and sat next to her.

She shuffled the cards and occasionally glanced around. "This is a fine room."

I nodded toward the door that led to the king's room. "Adjoining chambers." With guards always posted outside.

She merely shrugged and dealt the cards while I silently wished to be situated farther from the king, where the distance would afford me more freedom.

Unable to concentrate, I stared at my hand. "The king may have any girl he pleases, yet he chose me. Why do you suppose?"

Mrs. Benton tilted her head. "Do you mean other than the obvious—your raven hair and alabaster skin?"

I exhaled and flopped back against the back of the settee in a very unladylike manner. "Surely, a man picks a wife with more than just beauty in mind."

"He may be only a baron to the humans of England, but to us he is still a king. If you had ruled our kind for hundreds of years, how would you choose? A man needs something pretty to look at if he plans to keep the wife for eternity."

"I cannot help envying the plain girls for their liberties." I sighed, giving a wistful wave of my hand.

She raised one brow. "Because the plain ones are immune to arranged marriages?"

No, but they would not be given away to the werewolf king. Maybe if it were any other man who claimed me, I would not be so opposed.

From the first moment he glimpsed me in my village years ago, he had taken every opportunity to touch me—a pat on the knee, his hand too low on my back, a kiss on the cheek dangerously close to my mouth.

I had known him but a few hours when he requested that my parents release me into his care, so he could take me back to the castle. My father declined, insisting I reach werewolf maturity first. For that, I would be eternally grateful.

Since then, I had made it my business to pay attention to what kind of a man my future husband was. During his yearly visits to the village, I witnessed him speaking harshly to his servants and how quick he was to punish. Once, he had left with a hunting party and come back one man short with no apology or explanation to the dead man's grieving wife and three children.

Perhaps if I had entered into our marriage without knowledge of his abuse of those around him, I would have been content to create a life with him.

Or perhaps not. Even if the king possessed some manner of honor and compassion, I would still have difficulty seeing past his violent opposition to trimming and cleaning his beard. I could only imagine the vile things the hair concealed. Perhaps his rancid smell emanated from there.

"If only he desired an heir like human kings. In that case, he would look to a human who could give him one."

Mrs. Benton gave me a sad smile. "King Mortimer has no use for an heir since he believes he will live and rule forever."

Forever was a very long time to have a man such as he ruling our kind. I shuddered as a light tap sounded at the door. "Come in."

A servant entered, carrying a tray. She set it nearby and prepared two cups of tea, then handed one to me.

"Thank you." I offered the girl a smile. She only lowered her eyes farther and dipped gracefully at the knees before shuffling out of the room.

"As for His Majesty's reason for choosing you..." Mrs. Benton laid her cards facedown. "King Mortimer loathes fragility. A born werewolf, like yourself, will start out stronger. And he prefers a mate who has been raised a werewolf and is accustomed to our ways over marrying a human who is turned, but clings to her humanity."

"If he sees humanity as a weakness, I must wonder why he ever looked my way." I reached out for the cards, then switched to silent communication. *Once he is my husband and realizes I am overflowing with compassion, he will see his mistake. How long will I keep my head then?* I met her gaze. *I have come here to die, have I not?*

Do not be silly, dear. She nudged aside the cards and leaned toward me. *He chose you because you are worthy of his affections and will make a fine queen.*

You and I both know the king is wrong and I will fail. Not only would I fail him and my new subjects, but also Mrs. Benton. I dropped my gaze to my lap to hide my burning eyes. *I shall displease him and be dead within a week of our nuptials.*

You will live up to his expectations, Mrs. Benton insisted, *if you put some effort into it.*

I picked up my cards, but could not see them through my blurred vision. *I cannot be happy with a man I am unable to love and I am most certain that I will never love King Mortimer.*

Unfortunately, my dear Hannah, you have no choice. She sighed, shaking her head as she picked up her own hand. *I must say, I am not surprised to learn of your feelings on this matter. I have suspected as much since the first day the king sent me to you years ago, but I beg you to try to curb your feelings. To defy the king will mean your death and I doubt my heart would survive that. I implore you to find a way to reconcile yourself to a life here as queen.*

If only I could. I raised my chin and met her gaze, my stomach sinking at the thought of disappointing my only true friend.

CHAPTER TWO

I HAD TO make Mrs. Benton understand. If she were to mention my feelings to the king, he may watch me more closely and I might never escape.

I am nothing but a possession to him and you cannot believe otherwise. And what if I fall in love one day? Since I will already be married, it will be impossible to be with the one I love. Eternity is an awful long time to be unhappy, do you not think?

You will take brief moments of happiness and cling to them. She gave me a sympathetic smile. *And you will live.*

That is not living. I slapped my cards against the table and pressed my lips together. *I will escape before the wedding and if I die in the attempt, then so be it. At least in death, I will be free.*

Mrs. Benton lowered her head so I could no longer read her expression. I waited, my muscles bunching with tension. I prayed she would not abandon me for my willful behavior.

I see your mind is set. Her chin trembled. She pushed her cards aside and rounded the table to embrace me.

We stood there, holding each other for a long moment, then she released me and raised a vertical index finger to her lips. *Though I may be sending you to an early grave, you might stay alive longer with assistance. What I am about to show you will not be enough, mind you, since escaping will not only require knowledge of the castle, but weapons and a store of food. None of which will be available to you tonight. Promise me you will be patient and wait for the right time.*

I nodded.

I pray that I will have a few weeks with you before you set on your journey. She squeezed my shoulders and nodded toward the wardrobe. *For what I am about to show you, you will need to wear something warm.*

Of course, I returned. If she planned to lead me past the guards and outside, why did we need to be quiet when the guards were sure to see us? I grabbed two cloaks, slipped into one, and handed her the other.

Thank you, child. Mrs. Benton shrugged on the borrowed cloak, then made certain both doors were locked and swept across the room to the far corner. Unsure why she had abandoned our only exit if we were soon to be outside, I hung back.

It is imperative that we not make a sound. She ran her hand along the wall, stopping at a spot shoulder level. She strained against the wall that finally gave way when she flattened her palms against it and shoved hard. Jerking her head, she motioned for me to follow.

I squeezed through the opening and she pulled

the panel behind me. The dank corridor smelled of rotting vermin and droppings.

Through the pitch-black, with my werewolf vision, I could make out Mrs. Benton's shape. As if sensing I had questions, she shook her head. Silent communication was convenient, but it created an energy that could be sensed by other werewolves. Most likely, it would not be detected past the stone walls, but Mrs. Benton obviously wanted to err on the side of caution.

We paused. I could hear King Mortimer's voice—and a woman's—coming from the other side of the wall.

When the servant had shown me to my room earlier, the door to the king's suite had been open. The servant had hurriedly closed it, but not before I got a quick peek of the layout. His bed was located on the other side of the wall near where I now stood. Which meant that both he and the woman were on his bed.

As his betrothed, I should have been outraged by a woman's presence in his chambers, but all I could manage was relief that it was she in his bed and not me. I shivered, trying not to imagine what they were doing. Mrs. Benton grimaced, echoing my sentiments.

We crept along the dark, narrow passageway for what seemed the entire length of the castle. Our pace slowed by our effort to be quiet, we finally rounded a corner and came upon a stairwell. We descended the tight space, the toes of our shoes gingerly feeling our way over the hard dirt.

Knowing the king could not possibly sense us

now, I asked, *How did you know these tunnels existed?*

My grandfather discovered them about two hundred years ago, she told me. *He took care with whom he shared this knowledge. Even His Majesty is ignorant of their existence. We must keep it that way if you are to survive this.*

If I were to survive it... I was at great risk being in the tunnels and now so was Mrs. Benton. On the day I escaped successfully, the king would seek out and punish anyone who helped. After this night, I would not speak of my upcoming escape to Mrs. Benton again. The less she knew, the safer she would be. I loved her too much to risk her life any more than I already had.

You have been in the king's service most of your life. I wonder why you would keep the knowledge of these tunnels to yourself, I said.

I am loyal to my kind and he is our king. Mrs. Benton turned to the right and I followed. *But I have witnessed too many injustices during his reign. To sit idly by, when I can be of assistance, well, I could not live with myself.*

The minutes stretched as we made our way, inch-by-inch, until we finally hit level floor again.

You have helped others?

She drew a heavy breath. *Yes and no. I have attempted to save many over the centuries, but only a handful have survived.*

My stomach lurched at the realization that I might end up being one of the many, not the few. But I had to try.

Mrs. Benton guided me down another long corridor and we climbed one more flight of steps. We paused at the landing to check for other werewolves who might be nearby.

I hear nothing. She carefully removed a stone from the wall and peered through the opening. Letting her fingertips guide her until she hit wood, she lifted a plank, then another, and squeezed through.

A rat scampered at my feet. I shuddered and followed Mrs. Benton out of the tunnel. By the scent of hay and horses, we were in the granary.

The servants have likely retired for the night. She held my hand and kept me close. *But we cannot be too careful.*

Mrs. Benton motioned me toward the window and we tiptoed over. Several yards away near the drawbridge, lanterns glowed as a lone guard staggered like he had indulged in too much spirits. A dog yapped at his feet and beyond them, down the hill in the distance, was a clump of trees.

If we go back the way we came, there is a tunnel that will lead across the courtyard to the smithy. She met my gaze, giving me a stern look. *But you will leave that for another day when you have more time to examine the king's swords and bows.*

Weapons! I had to steal what I needed and hide them. When the time came for me to flee, I would only have to travel the tunnels, then climb through the window and freedom would be mine.

Careful in your haste, milady, Mrs. Benton warned

as if reading my mind. *Do not be so anxious that you do not take a fast horse and provisions. Also, weapons will do you little good if you know not how to use them. Most of all, you must have a very good plan for getting past the guards.* She gave my hand a comforting squeeze.

Yes, I needed to think about those things. I had never been more thankful for her and our friendship. If I managed to escape and survive, I would miss her terribly.

She tugged on my hand. *We must hurry back, in case a servant comes to tend you and informs the king of your absence.*

We took the same route back, past the planks, down the steps and up again, and through the musty corridor. Mrs. Benton halted in front of the narrow wooden door to my room before slipping through. I followed.

Inside, she sat at the foot of my bed and motioned me over to take the spot next to her. "Is your room to your liking?"

I obeyed, giving Mrs. Benton a knowing look. She was making conversation for any eavesdroppers, like the guards just outside my door, so they would know we were still there and all was well. "Yes, thank you."

"His Majesty will expect you to break fast with him. Afterward, a hunting party will leave and he will be among them. You will have to find a way to amuse yourself until his return that evening."

Oh, yes, I could surely find a way to occupy my time. With the king gone, perhaps no one would notice if I kept to myself... or rummaged through his room—assuming I could slip by my handmaidens. I might even find something to aid in my escape.

Mrs. Benton and I played several games of cards, then she retired for the evening, but not before a word of warning. *You must learn your way around, to be sure, but use caution. If one of his guards catches your scent where you should not be, you will lose the king's trust and be watched even more closely.*

She paused, her lips thinning as she grasped my shoulders. *Remember, my child, you mustn't trust another soul with your knowledge of the tunnels or you may risk your freedom forever. If they are discovered, you may not find another way. I regret that this must be my only act toward aiding you in this endeavor for I have risked too much already.*

Of course, I said. *I will not involve you further. And I appreciate what you have done. Without you, I may not have found a way.*

What you have will not be enough, but you are in no hurry. His Majesty will not take you as his wife for another four weeks.

Only one month. Not much time at all.

CHAPTER THREE

AFTER MRS. BENTON left, I waited a few minutes before wrapping myself in a cloak again and slipping into the tunnel. I doubted she would approve of another outing that evening, but the sooner I could formulate an escape plan, the sooner I would be free of the king. And as our wedding day neared, he would likely guard me more closely, not less. I had not a moment to lose.

I would learn those tunnels well enough to travel them in a fraction of the time Mrs. Benton and I had. When I left the castle for good, I would be long gone by the time the king and his guards realized I was missing.

As I crept down the long passageway, I silently fumed at my parents. When my father shook hands with the werewolf king four years ago, he was elevated from pack leader to Baron. I had been sold—no better than a slave or peasant—in exchange for a small fortune once the wedding took place.

Since the moment my fate had been sealed, my father gloated over his elevated status, thrilled he would no longer need to hunt to feed his family. My mother behaved no better as she exulted over the honor that His Majesty had bestowed upon her family by taking me as his bride—and the beneficial connections she would make.

Arranged marriages were commonplace. A woman being treated as a possession was not unheard of. It infuriated me nonetheless. My parents had traded my happiness for theirs. If not for them using me as a bargaining tool, I would not be here at all. I would be back in our village, very likely quite poor, but free to marry whomever I chose.

I could not help but wonder how the members of our pack would have behaved toward me had they not known I would be their future queen. Would the young men have looked at me differently, instead of living in fear of offending the king? Would the girls still have been my friends? More accurately, were they ever my friends at all?

And if I had not been given my own personal guards wherever I went, what other opportunity might have presented itself? If I had not been promised to the king or if the pack had been kept ignorant of who I was to become, I might've had a chance at a normal life—get my first kiss behind the well, or fall in love.

Two things I knew with absolute certainty: I could never love King Mortimer and I would not be his queen.

At last, I reached the door to the granary. Just as Mrs. Benton had done earlier that evening, my hand brushed over the wall in search of the loose stone. Before removing it, I paused to see if I could hear other werewolves nearby, then I peered through the opening. After locating the planks, my heart pounded as I set them down and slipped out of the tunnel and into the granary.

I could not allow myself to be distracted and get caught. The instant I realized a werewolf was nearby, he would be aware of me, too. If he found my scent, he would recognize it the next time he encountered me. I could not allow that to happen. In the future, I would only wander late at night when there was less risk of being seen, and stick to wide open spaces, when possible, to dilute my scent.

After tiptoeing to the window, I crouched and peered out. Not a soul in sight, but that did not mean no one was nearby. I would have to move so fast that no one would see me.

My pulse raced as I braced myself.

From this vantage point I had a view of the spot where I had seen the blond blacksmith that morning. I imagined him as he had looked, his sculpted jaw and the sharp angle of his nose. Mostly, I remembered his deep blue eyes.

His work space would surely have weapons, but would it be wise to search there tonight, leaving my scent for him to discover? I would never get close enough to the slave for him to know it had been me snooping through his tools.

I closed my eyes and concentrated as I inhaled deeply, checking again for any werewolf energy or scents. Finding none, I climbed through the window, raced across the cobblestones in a flash, and slipped inside the dark building. My werewolf vision adjusted quickly and I crept soundlessly to a workbench laden with iron bars that would one day be made into swords.

Beyond the bench, horseshoes lined the walls, along with various metal tools. My gaze shifted to the next wall to see various sizes of daggers and smaller knives. After checking over my shoulder to be sure no one had come in, I grabbed one of the knives and slipped it into my bodice.

Visiting the smithy again would be too risky, so anything I wanted had to be taken now. My eyes scanned a long, wooden table. A bow lay on the end and a quiver hung on a hook nearby.

The women in my village were not allowed to learn about weapons. Our job was to prepare meals, mend clothes and keep house. But since the day I had learned about my betrothal to the king, I had made it a point to touch my father's bow in his presence, so my scent would not alert him later after I snuck away with it to practice. Winning in any tournaments was unlikely, but when I aimed, I usually hit my target. My arrow might not kill an attacker, but it would slow him down.

Staring at the bow, I knew I would need it since the dagger in my bodice would not be enough. If I stole the bow, where would I stow it? I could not risk being caught with it in my room. I had no idea who else had knowledge of the tunnels and could not take a chance that someone would find anything I left there. However, if I buried the bow in the forest, it would be waiting for me when I escaped.

With trembling fingers, I lifted the bow, then snagged a quiver and crammed it full with arrows. After examining the selection of swords, I chose a shorter one that could be hidden in my clothing, then I located a matching scabbard and hung both around my waist under my robes.

Now I just had to make it to the trees.

The king had guards posted around the castle. Some might even be out in the woods. When I slowed to find a place to hide the weapons, they would easily see me. My heart slammed against my ribcage. But I had to do it and could not delay.

I might die before I ever had a chance to use the weapons. At the very least, I hoped to hide them before anyone discovered me, since having them in my possession would be difficult to explain.

As to why I had wandered outside the castle walls, perhaps I could say that I needed to morph and wanted more space than the bailey provided. If the guard scolded me for not bringing a chaperon, I would say that I had never needed one back in the village. Unfortunately, those excuses would only work one time. I needed to make this excursion to the forest count.

After a check to make sure no guards lurked nearby, I jumped from the smithy window and raced toward the trees, moving faster than I ever had in my life. Once under the cover of the forest, I stood absolutely still and listened for any werewolves who might have followed me. There were none.

But something else was out there. I could sense

its energy.

I spun, my heart pounding against my ribs, my stomach fluttering at the sight of the beautiful blond blacksmith standing a yard away.

His eyes narrowed as his gaze swept over me. "The bow, quiver and arrows... I believe they belong to me."

My mouth dropped open. Why had I not been aware he was following me? A scent drifted to me, but I could not place it. Sweet with a hint of earth.

"I saw you leave the smithy." He nodded toward the quiver slung over my shoulder. "My father made those for me when I was twelve and the arrows were carved by my hand. I would be most grateful if you would return them, milady."

I glanced at the bow and quiver, unwilling to give them up. I *needed* them. "I regret I am unable to relinquish them, sir, but I shall be happy to compensate you for your trouble."

His stance remained respectful with his head bowed, but his words were clipped. "My father's gifts are not for sale."

Letting the weapons go was not an option, though. As a werewolf, especially a born one, I had the advantage of strength against shape-shifters. Still, I did not want to take any chances. I raised my chin and angled my shoulder so he could not easily snatch the bow. "I shall do everything in my power to return your belongings once I have no use for them. I am afraid, sir, that is my only offer."

He waited a beat, then dropped his voice to a low

growl. "Surely your betrothed is wealthy enough to provide for all your needs."

"Give a woman a weapon?" I laughed, but it was devoid of humor.

His brows rose. "Which begs the obvious question."

Yes, why did I need the bow? How would I possibly explain that? My gaze dropped to his feet.

He cleared his throat. "He has no knowledge of you being here, nor that you feel the need to possess weapons."

I saw no point in denying it. Stretching taller, I trained my eyes on his and studied his face for any sign that he might fight me for the bow. He just stood there with arms folded over his chest, staring at me.

"I give you my word that I will find a way to return your things, once I am able," I said.

He gave a short laugh. "That will not do. Meet me here tomorrow and you shall have another bow and quiver—which are not gifts from my father."

I took a step back as I contemplated his offer. I saw few options. If he planned to betray me, very likely I could not change his mind anyway. "And what of our meeting? You will not speak of our conversation or that you saw me tonight?"

"You have my word." He sighed and ran a hand through his hair, then refocused on me. "I am Eli."

Could I trust him? His strength would be no match against mine, and the sword within my robes guaranteed victory. But if I killed him, everyone would smell my scent on him. I could cry to the king how Eli had intended to hurt me, but that would be a lie. I would say just about anything to save my own life, but what if Eli meant to keep his word? I would have murdered an innocent man.

What choice did I have but to rely upon his promise?

Fear rose up in my throat and I swallowed it down. "Hannah."

"It is my honor, milady." Eli bowed and stepped back, his gaze locking on mine.

Something about his deep voice sent warmth spreading through my middle. Becoming fascinated by a shape-shifter — or any man at all — was a terrible idea. I needed to get away from him.

I turned to go, then froze. "Why did I not sense you until you were close? I should have sensed you were nearby when I was in the smithy."

"I am a shape-shifter." His mouth twisted up at the corners.

Pressing my own into a thin line, I struggled to ignore the quickening of my pulse. "I am afraid my experience has been limited to my former pack and the occasional human."

"We do not possess the same strength as were-wolves, nor do we emit the same energy. Therefore, we are not as easily detected." Eli skulked toward me, getting closer until I felt the heat radiating off his skin. "Even like this, my scent is weak. You can sense me, of course, but it is different than what you feel standing next to a werewolf. Your betrothed, for instance."

No, nothing at all like what I had felt when I had

been with the king earlier. I studied Eli's handsome face and reminded myself not to allow his good looks to distract me. My attraction to him was not worth risking my life. Or his.

"Quite an advantage. If you can take a werewolf by surprise, I wonder why you are allowed to roam free."

Eli's eyes darkened. "His Majesty knows I will never leave or do anything to harm him and his people."

"But why, when you have freedom within your grasp, do you not take it?" I tilted my head.

One second passed, then two before he replied, "You should go before a guard sees you. I will meet you here same time tomorrow and we shall make a trade."

Apparently, he expected me to keep his belongings and return with them tomorrow. But if he betrayed me, the king would learn of my whereabouts this evening, and the weapons in my possession would prove the shape-shifter spoke the truth. Without the weapons, it was the shifter's word against mine.

On the other hand, if he kept his word and told no one he saw me, he would also keep his word and bring me another bow. Either way, I had no need for his things.

I took a deep breath and handed him his bow and quiver. "Tomorrow then."

Eli stared at the bow, then shifted his focus to me. "Thank you, milady." He bowed his head, then swung away and vanished into the night.

Following his example and returning to my room would have been wise, but I needed to make use of every precious moment outside the castle. I had to learn of every raised root that might trip me and every ditch that might swallow me. Then, when it was time for me to run, nothing would slow me down.

CHAPTER FOUR

JUST AFTER SUNRISE, Mrs. Benton spoke from the other side of my chamber door. "It is I, milady."

My scratchy eyes opened with great effort. The last thing I wanted to do was spend my morning in the company of the king. If only I could claim fatigue from the prior day's travel and skip breakfast. But since I had retired early the night before, His Majesty would assume I had spent that time sleeping and therefore required no more. Instead, I had used my allotted rest time to consort with a shape-shifter.

A flash of Eli's handsome face came to mind. The king's guards had not dragged me from my chambers in the wee hours, which meant Eli had kept my confidence—even though I had stolen his bow. I scarcely knew him and already believed this shape-shifter was worth ten King Mortimers.

I could not imagine Eli feeling any loyalty toward the king who treated him as though he owned him. So why did he stay? I sighed. Resigned to having breakfast with infinitely inferior company, I pushed off the bed and opened the door.

Mrs. Benton offered me a smile, but it faded on closer inspection. *Dear child, have you been up all night?* she asked silently.

Not the entire night. I moved to my wardrobe for a gown, snatched one and held it up for her approval.

"That will do." She rested her hands on my shoulder and met my gaze. *I warned you to use caution with the tunnels. It is dangerous. Many of the king's laws may be disagreeable, but I have a good life here— better than I would fare outside the castle. You must know that if you get caught, I must claim complete ignorance.*

And I would help her stay ignorant of my activities by not disclosing my previous contact with the slave. I squeezed her hand. *If they catch me, no matter what I say, my punishment will be death. If I stay, I believe my soul shall slowly die. 'Tis the same either way, so I shall do as I please. However, I promise to take your involvement to the grave.*

My greatest fear is that it might come to that. She gave me a sad smile. "Let's get you ready for breakfast."

After Mrs. Benton helped me into my gown, a handmaiden arrived and braided my hair. She tied it with ribbon, bowed and left.

"You are the most beautiful girl there ever was," Mrs. Benton declared as she tucked away a few strands of my hair.

But had I not been so beautiful, the king would not have chosen me as his wife and I would not be planning an escape and risking my life. The image of

Eli's face swam before me again and, for the first time, I wished I did not have to leave. Had I not belonged to the king...

"Thank you." I smiled, wishing I could take Mrs. Benton with me on the run. But as she had pointed out, she had a good life working for the king. Being hunted and possibly killed for betraying the king was not something I wanted for her anyway.

Someone stirred in the chamber next door. King Mortimer would leave directly after breakfast and be gone all day — the perfect opportunity for me to rifle through his things. He might have maps in his room or letters or something that might give me information on his plans and help me to decide my path once I made it outside the castle grounds. He might even have a weapon that would go unnoticed if it disappeared.

In order not to get caught, though, I needed to get into his room while he was still there. Then, when I returned while he was away and he picked up my scent later, he would assume it was from my earlier visit.

"You go ahead. I will be down shortly."

Once Mrs. Benton left, I listened at the door to the king's room. Hearing footfalls and the rustling of robes, I tapped on the door. A moment later, it swung open.

"Your Majesty." I curtsied and offered a shy smile. Inwardly, I cringed, hating to give him the impression that he pleased me in any way. "I wondered if you would escort me to mass."

He smiled back and held out his arm for me to loop mine through. "It happens that I am on my way there now."

I crossed the threshold, closed the door behind me and took his arm. The king moved forward and I pulled back, bending over to adjust my skirt. The longer I stayed in his room, the more scent I would leave behind.

After a moment, I straightened. "You are too kind."

As the king paraded me down the hallway that led to the chapel, I felt owned. Property. I strived to stifle the urge to flinch from his touch.

"Two new recruits have joined our ranks this past week. Once the older pup is trained, I will send him to Scotland to help control some shape-shifter rebels. The other is quite skilled in sword fighting. I am considering adding him to my army here."

A man rarely discussed business with a female. I was absolutely certain the king's only objective was to demonstrate his power over others. "I am sure they are honored that you think so highly of them, milord." I willed my mouth to stay shut, so I would not undo my hard work by speaking my mind. I could not imagine living the rest of my life being forced to tolerate his arrogance. With each step toward the chapel, I became more and more certain of my decision: I would escape or die trying.

At last, we settled onto one of the pews and I could look straight ahead without having to speak to him.

After mass, I accompanied him to the great hall

where everyone gathered for the first meal of the day. The large room was crowded and noisy as we took our places at the head of the table. Once the king introduced me to everyone at his table—two of his advisors and several knights—he barely acknowledged my existence, except to occasionally leer at me or pat my hand between gulps of ale from his goblet. My skin crawled each time he touched me. Unfortunately, I could not yank my hand from his grasp and reveal my feelings.

His departure with the hunting party would be most welcome.

After the roasted pig had been devoured, the king mounted his horse, promising to return by sundown. The moment he rode through the castle gates on his steed, I slipped away to my room. Lying on the bed, my gaze kept drifting to the door that connected to his room. If someone were in there, I would not be able to sense him or her beyond the wall.

Standing at the door, I listened carefully, but heard nothing. If anyone were to see me, I could claim to be looking for a lost pin from earlier that morning. I was willing to risk getting caught in favor of the benefits of rifling through his things.

The door gave way as soon I turned the knob and I slipped through to the other side. I had no idea what to look for or what might be useful. I only knew I needed to be quick in case anyone came in.

Everything was as I had seen it before breakfast, yet there was something else. Like the night before when I had been speaking with Eli.

I took a turn around the room. Ah, a shape-shifter was close by. I could feel him. Or her. But where? Likely, the shifter already knew of my presence, which put me at a grave disadvantage.

I quickly scanned the area, my eyes landing on a small cage by the fireplace. I crept closer. A gray rat stared up at me with tiny black eyes through thin gaps between the thick metal bars. Too small for a rat to slip through.

Why did the king keep a shape-shifter in his room? I wondered why the rat did not shift into a smaller animal and slip past the narrow opening.

A memory flashed through my mind of my father years before, bragging how he had captured one. The shape-shifter had turned into a small dog in hopes that my father would not notice he was a shifter. My father had drawn his sword and held it against the shifter's throat as he stuffed him in a large pot, then weighed down the lid.

A shape-shifter could change into anything he wanted, as often as he liked. But before each new shape, he must always become human. Confined within the iron pot, the shifter was trapped as a dog.

A pang of nausea swirled in my stomach at the unjust treatment of the weaker species and remembering how my father had gloated over his triumph. Just as a werewolf was part human, so was a shape-shifter. They were no more inferior to a werewolf for lacking strength, than a woman was inferior to a man for the same reason.

As I stared at what looked like a common rat, I could hear its tiny heartbeat accelerate. And I could sense it was a female. *I will not hurt you, I promise,* I told her. But I could not help her either. I was not sure I could save myself, much less someone else. If I could find a way, though, I would.

I tiptoed to the bureau and eyed gold coins spilling from a satchel. I had nearly a month before I had to leave. I had no need to take anything yet, not when its absence might create suspicion. Would he miss just one coin, though? It might be useful in paying Eli for the replacement bow later tonight.

I moved onto the wardrobe, but none of its contents caught my interest. After another quick glance at the shifter, I returned to my own room. I locked the door behind me, wishing I knew nothing of the shapeshifter in the cage.

† † †

By the time the king returned late that night, silence had already settled in the castle. Slowing my breathing, I lay unmoving in my bed so he would assume I slept. I waited until he had been soundless in his chambers — and hopefully asleep — for over an hour before slipping the sword into the waistband of my skirt and covering it with my cloak. After traveling through the tunnel, I headed to the woods to meet Eli for the bow and quiver.

In a moment of curiosity, I turned right toward the king's room. Muffled voices met me where the stone wall stopped and planks began. I thanked the heavens that the king had no knowledge of the secret passageway or that he, too, probably had access from his room.

Knowing the wooden wall blocked him from sensing me just as well as a stone wall, I crept closer and laid my ear against the wood—which carried sound infinitely better than stone.

"We kill her, then blame it on the shifter," the king said in a low voice.

"No one will believe it," a woman rebutted. She sounded like the same one I had heard in his chamber the night before. "How will you convince our people that a shifter would dare murder your wife?"

I sucked in a breath. Murder *me?*

CHAPTER FIVE

"MY DEAREST, YOU must have faith," the king said. I could almost hear the smile in his voice. "I have something the shifter wants. When he realizes he shall never have it, he will become quite distraught, and his fury will be so complete, he will be driven to revenge by taking the life of the one I love most. My new bride." He chuckled. "At least that is the story I shall tell."

The person he loved most. Yes, and that was why he was planning my demise. I drew in a shaky breath and concentrated on their voices.

She gave a low, throaty purr. "The news will travel and werewolves across the country will take their anger out on shape-shifters. You shall have your war, my dear. Hundreds of shape-shifters will die and they will never be a threat to us again."

The king chuckled. "You will comfort me in my time of grief and once my mourning is over, I will declare my love for you and we shall marry."

"And be together as we were meant to be," she said, her voice becoming fainter.

Something bumped against the wall, just on the

other side where I stood. I jolted, but quickly steadied myself when I remembered they could not sense me. A low moan signaled the end of their conversation and I backed away.

† † †

The cool night air stung my cheeks, but the still of the forest calmed me as I scanned for the spot where I had seen Eli the night before. Inhaling deeply, I searched for his scent.

But he was not there. I was sure of it.

With time to spare, I examined the shrubs and rocks, looking for the perfect place to stow a bow and quiver. After a few minutes, I found a boulder wedged over a raised tree root. Under it was a space large enough to hide my weapons. I shoved the sword and scabbard inside, then covered the opening with leaves.

Just as I rose, a twig snapped. I spun to find a tall figure about two yards away.

Eli.

My heart thumped faster.

His eyes narrowed. "Surely you do not fear me."

"Of course not. You took me by surprise is all," I replied. Over his shoulder sat the strap of a quiver and in his hand, he held a bow. I reached into my cloak pocket and withdrew the gold piece I had taken from the king's room. "For your trouble."

He shoved the bow and quiver toward me, but did not take my payment. "I have no use for gold. If I am caught with that, the king might question how I obtained it and I can offer no explanation."

"Hide the gold and use it when you are free," I said.

He shook his head. "I will never be free."

How was that possible? Had he no hope of escape? None at all? "There is always a way."

"No one has ever escaped and survived for long. The king's men do not stop until they find their quarry, and then proof of their death is stuck on a pike upon the guard's return."

My brows furrowed. "You mean their heads?"

He gave me a grim smile. "Yes, they are displayed just outside the castle walls as a reminder for anyone else who considers defying the king. In the three years I have been here, the few who left against the king's wishes all returned dead."

I considered that a moment as I examined my new bow. "We are all slaves or prisoners," I murmured.

"It is only seen as a prison to those who wish to leave."

I thought of Mrs. Benton. "I suppose some could be happy here."

"Yes," Eli agreed. "But you are not?"

I laughed without humor. "Being forced to marry a man I do not love is reason enough not to be, I should think."

"Drowning in riches and servants cannot make *you* forget?" One side of his mouth curled up.

I held up the bow. "Does living in a castle make you forget?"

His eyes darkened as he took a step toward me.

"You should not attempt to leave. Any woman would be overjoyed to be in your position. Accept him as your husband, take his gifts and *live*."

Eli was so sure I would not survive if I left. But I now knew I would not survive if I stayed. "He plans to kill me and make it appear someone else did it."

When the king mentioned blaming my death on the shifter, had he meant Eli? If so, Eli would be killed as well. He had kept his promise and brought me a bow and he had not given me away. Slave or not, he deserved to know what the king intended.

Except... the king valued Eli as a blacksmith, which is why he forced him to stay. Surely, he would not kill Eli just to start a war. Perhaps the king had another shifter in mind. But if Eli really was the shifter the king had meant and I told Eli what I had heard, would he try to escape and get himself killed? I barely knew him, but I could not bear the thought of him dying if I could prevent it.

If he had no knowledge of being part of the king's plan, he would never need to risk anything. And if I escaped successfully, the king would have nothing to blame on Eli and he would be safe.

I did not want to leave, but good sense told me it was time to move on. I just needed Eli gone so I could put the bow and quiver away for later. Eli was a slave and, according to the king and all other werewolves, he was beneath me. But I knew better. From what I had witnessed so far, Eli was better than most, if not all, werewolves I had met.

Eli jerked his head toward the castle. "If you were to try and escape, you could slip away into the forest without being seen. But once you are out of the woods, you must get past guards and traps."

"Traps?" My stomach twisted. "You know where they lay?"

He lifted a shoulder. "Yes, but you would still need to get past the guards."

"Run fast enough and they will not see me," I said.

He shook his head. "Everyone leaves behind a scent. You may get by them at first, but they would no doubt find you. The king's guards are excellent trackers."

"They might smell *me*, but perhaps *your* scent is not strong enough. You could easily evade them," I said. "You would not even have to run. Just spread your wings and fly."

His mouth formed into a hard line. "If I leave, *she* will die."

I should not have felt such disappointment at the mention of a girl or be saddened that he belonged to another. I barely knew Eli. Besides, he was a shifter. Even if he could feel anything for me, neither of us could ever act on it. We would be shunned and vilified anywhere we went. If we survived an escape.

I took a deep breath and focused. "That is why you can never leave? Because he holds your loved one hostage?"

His chin dropped and his shoulder slumped. "Yes."

"But you cannot just give up," I said. "There is always a way."

"Possibly. Unfortunately, I have yet to discover it." His spine straightened, his eyes hardening. "But I shall never give up on her."

I hoped she was not trapped in a pot, like the dog that my dad had caught.

Wait... the rat in the king's chambers... could that shifter be his beloved? My eyes stung in horror and my stomach churned. "I must go."

Every part of me screamed to run from the king right then and keep on running until I was free. But I could not. After this conversation with Eli, I knew I must not attempt an escape without a very good plan.

No longer caring if Eli knew where I hid the bow, I lifted the branch, slid the bow under the boulder, then swept the leaves and brush back under the rock. I turned and left without another word.

Once in my chamber, I pulled the dagger from my bodice and slipped it under my pillow so I could easily reach it. With the king plotting against me, I could not take any chances. Given his age and strength, he would easily overpower me, but a weapon might take him by surprise and afford me a chance to run. I needed any advantage I could get.

† † †

The next morning, the werewolf king held out his arm and I slipped mine through his. All eyes followed us as he swaggered down the long hallway toward the great hall.

"How are you settling into your new home?" he

asked. "I trust you are finding everything to your liking."

"Yes, I am in want of nothing, Your Majesty." I peered over at him and smiled. It would not do for him to know I had learned of his treachery. "I am acutely aware of the great honor you have bestowed upon me."

"Very well." He patted my arm and grinned, his yellow teeth just visible beyond his long beard. "Let us dine."

Everyone bowed as we entered the great hall. Once we took our chairs at the table, the chattering resumed and I tried to look busy with my gown to avoid eye contact with the king. But I could not put him off for long or he might become suspicious.

With tremendous effort, I met the king's gaze. "I understand Prince Edward will be calling on us any day."

"Yes, the Prince of Wales and his family take immense pleasure in their own importance. They will arrive, and I will smile and present his family with gifts. After a while, they will be reassured of their great superiority and leave me to my business."

"I cannot help but wonder why you allow the humans to rule." Though I had to pretend to support him, I prayed a man such as he would never rule over humans. "Surely, there is a way for you to take your rightful place?"

He brushed a finger under my chin. "Naïve girl. In order to triumph over humans, I would need to increase my army. The higher the werewolf population, the greater risk of losing my throne. Another werewolf could rule and reap the benefits of my hard work."

"Very clever." I smiled. "This way, you maintain all control over our kind."

"Exactly. The humans are rarely a bother. They seldom travel the eighty miles to visit. When they do, they stay a few days and take their leave." The corner of his mouth curled up. "I have my ways of dealing with those who believe themselves to be above me."

His ways of dealing with them probably involved blackmail or other such devices. I could only imagine the secrets my king could gather by coercing a shape-shifter disguised as a pet into the royal castle. Intrigue was the last thing I wanted to worry about though. I had enough on my mind just figuring out how to escape with my life. And when I succeeded, the king would be but a memory.

"I must compliment you on your fine gardens," I told him. "I have never seen anything like them."

He gathered my hand into his and squeezed. "When you are my queen, this will all be yours, my dearest Hannah."

For only an instant before he murdered me. Inside, I seethed, my free hand clenching into a fist. I wondered if the king would prefer to do it himself or have someone else kill me while he was out with a hunting party. I suspected he would choose the latter where he may provide himself an alibi. So long as no one doubts the king's innocence, he can blame it on the shape-shifters and he would have his war.

And Eli... how would he find death? Would his head be on a pike outside the castle walls as an example for any would-be traitors? What about his beloved, who was trapped in a cage and could be killed so easily? That, I felt certain, was a task the king would save for himself.

My throat constricted at the thought. Was there no way to save her? Save Eli? Likely not.

CHAPTER SIX

PRINCE EDWARD ARRIVED the next morning and my day was spent at the king's side, first at a jousting tournament, then the musicians entertained us during supper. I was rarely spoken to and my responses were almost never required. That was just as well, because the strain of pretending contentment had worn on me.

Much to my relief, Prince Edward and my king disappeared after the feast, which left me to find amusement on my own. I did not mind. I stopped in my chamber to shift into my wolf form, since showing our true selves in the bailey later and risk exposing ourselves to the humans would not do.

I shuddered to think what would happen if the human prince discovered he was in a castle full of werewolves. If word spread that we existed, armies upon armies would descend upon us. Though we were much stronger than humans, we were outnumbered more than a thousand to one. Surely they would hunt us to extinction. I could not wait until the guests departed so I could morph and run in the bailey.

Once I had run out the wolf cravings, I left my room to amble down the long, empty corridor toward the library. As I neared the doorway, the smell of leather and old parchment tickled my nose. Books lined the walls, to the very top of the high ceiling. I kept to the lower level since it took less effort and less commitment. I did not want to become engrossed, lose track of time and miss my chance to see Eli. Not that he would necessarily show. But if he did, I intended to be there in the woods.

As I ran my fingers over the rows of worn spines, my bones ached from exhaustion, stress and sleep deprivation. Werewolves healed quickly, but we still needed rest—though we needed much less than humans—to rebuild our strength. Tomorrow, I would feign fatigue and make up for lost sleep.

But tonight, I would roam the castle grounds via the tunnels. Later, I would go to the forest in search of Eli. He knew about the traps beyond the forest and the posted guards. What else did he know that might help me or his beloved?

My urge to tell him about the rat in the king's chamber nearly overpowered me. But if I revealed his love's location, would Eli put himself in danger to save her? My stomach churned at the thought. I would tell him before I fled the castle. For now, I just needed to see him and gather any information I could.

But I had to admit, at least to myself, Eli's assistance was not the only reason to seek him out. Two meetings and I had already grown attached—for bringing me a bow, advising me on my escape, and keeping my confidence. Mostly, I admired his loyalty. He knew the layout of the castle and grounds, knew the dangers that could befall him. If anyone could escape, it was he. Yet he did not. Because he would not leave his love.

I wished it was me he refused to abandon.

I shook my head, desperately rejecting those feelings. I barely knew the man. Besides, not only was he a shifter, he was already taken. As was I — to the king, no less.

Still, I longed to see him.

† † †

Luckily, humans needed more sleep than werewolves and retired early. And their poor vision made them even less likely to see me dashing into the forest. For now, only the guards worried me.

I ran through the trees, stopping where I stowed the bow and quiver, and blew out a breath in relief. Still there. This discovery bolstered my faith and trust in Eli.

Warm tingles spread through me when I sensed him. I turned slowly and met his gaze, offering him a tentative smile.

He did not return my greeting as he took a cautious step closer. "Hiding more weapons?"

"No."

"It is dangerous for you to be out, milady."

"I suppose it is." I bit my lip. "But I hoped you

might be willing to share anything else you know. The king believes you will never leave without your... wife? Comforted by that knowledge, perhaps he speaks freely around you."

"She is my sister."

I released a shaky breath. "Oh."

"Imparting much more information than I already have may not be wise, milady. I fear that if you know too much, you will come to believe you can do something that cannot be done. And you will be killed for attempting it."

"Unfortunately, I have no choice." I waited a breath. "I... overheard a conversation that was not meant for me."

His brows lifted expectantly.

"He means to kill me shortly after we marry."

Eli's forehead furrowed. "Why would he murder his own wife?"

"He intends to blame it on someone else." I gave a shaky laugh, knowing I should be more specific. But I hoped it would not come to that. I intended to escape before the king ever involved Eli. I never wanted him to be in my situation, faced with the choice of staying and dying or running and being hunted. His decision would be made more difficult since running would mean leaving his sister behind. "So you see, I have no choice but to go."

"I do not know why anyone would murder his own wife, yet after my dealings with him, I cannot doubt it. I will help you, if I can." He turned away from me and ran a hand through his straight, blond hair. "Several times a year, His Majesty travels for a fortnight amongst the villages in his realm, to inspect the land and collect taxes and such. This is to remind everyone of their true sovereign."

"Like what Prince Edward is doing now." Surely the castle will seem less like a prison with the king gone. "When will this trip take place?"

"He departs in about a week, soon after the prince is gone. Many of his men will go with him, which will leave the castle and grounds with fewer guards for you to get past."

I wanted to suggest that he, also, take advantage, but I already knew he would not leave his sister. In his shoes, I would not either. But I had to try. I inched toward him. "And less guards in your way as well."

He stood a breath away, eyes cast down toward me. They softened for a moment before hardening again. "You should not be here, much less plotting ways to get yourself killed." His jaw tightened when I did not move. "I have nothing else to offer, no other information. Do not come here again. If you get caught—"

"They will kill me?" I finished for him, standing my ground and lifting my chin. "No matter the path, that is my fate. And if you are right and they punish me with death, then I will be most pleased with a little conversation before I die." I waited to let him absorb that. "You may be one of only three people in the entire castle with no agenda."

"I cannot help you any more than I already have." He held out his hands and backed away. "You have no business with a shape-shifter."

The next moment I was alone.

† † †

The following morning, Mrs. Benton opened the drapes and gave me a withering look over her shoulder. *Please do not make me regret showing you the tunnels. I find myself lying awake worrying about you long after I should be asleep. I can only hope you are being clever while you risk your life.*

I propped myself up on my elbows. *I swear to you that I am taking all precautions. I am in no immediate danger. You have my word.*

Mrs. Benton squinted as though that would force the truth from me. "Let's get you dressed."

Once I was fit to be seen by my king and the Prince of Wales, I joined them for mass, then we feasted on roasted beef, fresh baked bread and vegetables from the king's garden. As usual, I was meant to be seen and appreciated from afar, but not heard.

Knowing the meal would drag on, I ate slowly to keep myself busy. After what seemed an eternity, the king rose from his chair. "Shall we make a trip to the smithy?"

My stomach flipped. I would see Eli. I could not speak with him in public, of course, but just laying eyes on him would be enough until after dark when I met him in the woods. If he showed up.

"As you wish," Prince Edward replied with a nod.

My king thrust out his elbow and I looped an arm through his. We made our way out of the great hall, paraded through the long corridor until finally, we met cobblestone outside. Eli stood in front of the smithy at the enormous slab of iron, a light breeze blowing his blond hair. The sleeves of his billowy white shirt were rolled up, the open collar showing tanned skin. He struck the hammer against the red hot metal of the sword and looked our way. My gaze met his and my blood hummed.

Your heart is beating wildly, my dear, the king told me silently. *Does this shape-shifter frighten you? If he bothers you in the slightest, I shall do away with him.*

No, milord, I answered, casting Eli a wary glance for the king's benefit. *I have never met one before and he is disconcerting. Just look at his clothes. Why, he is positively savage.*

The king patted my arm, still entwined with his. *He will not hurt you or anyone else. I have made sure of that.*

And I knew exactly how he had ensured everyone's safety. Or rather how he had rendered Eli harmless and unable to leave. My blood boiled at the king's cruelty, but as we stood near Eli, I struggled to keep my calm. It would not do for me to lose my temper, especially in front of our guests.

"Excuse me, my dear. I am sure His Highness would like to look at our fine swords," King Mortimer said.

I stepped aside and he motioned the prince to follow him into the smithy. All the guards went too, leaving me standing beside Eli. I could not stay but for a moment or risk drawing attention to myself.

The servants had not come with us, and the king and prince were too far away now to sense me speaking telepathically. *I hope you are well,* I told Eli.

Go with them, he ordered. *You must not take the chance that he will notice you are missing.*

I watched him from under my lashes as I pretended to arrange my gown. *You will be there tonight, yes?*

Absolutely not. He glared at me. *Stay in your chamber where you are safe.*

I cannot. I spun and dashed off to join the others. I hoped to see Eli later that night, but he had made his intentions clear. Deflated and dejected, I stepped into the dim light of the smithy and hugged the walls as my king bestowed a bejeweled sword upon the prince. Imparting gifts was certainly a brilliant way of manipulating royalty, although I guessed my king combined that with other methods of maintaining control.

† † †

After dinner, I retired to my chamber and morphed into my wolf form. I missed the space the bailey provided and could only hope our human guests departed soon.

As exhausted as I had become from lack of sleep, I belonged in bed. But for reasons I could not explain, I was drawn to Eli and could not stay away. I needed to see him. The fact that he could very well be the only one in the entire castle, other than his sister, who could identify with my situation only made me want to see him more. And I hoped that he might tell me something that could help me save her.

Once the castle quieted, I went to our spot in the woods. To pass the time waiting for Eli, I checked to make sure my bow and quiver were where I had left them, along with the sword and scabbard. Assured they were safe, I scanned the perimeter, wondering where the guard's traps might be laid. Nothing seemed out of the ordinary.

My limbs weighed heavy with the lateness of the hour. I needed rest. I promised myself I would stay in tomorrow and catch up on sleep. But if Eli did not show tonight, I would have to go out again tomorrow night. The next day, I would be absolutely ruined from sleep deprivation.

Exploring the woods, I stayed close by in case Eli appeared. Minutes stretched on and I could not afford to stay out any longer. I switched direction to head back to the castle and froze.

"Why are you here?"

Pivoting, I came face-to-face with Eli just three feet away. He scowled, his body rigid and motionless.

I shrugged. "I have more questions."

He shook his head and backed away. "Go."

CHAPTER SEVEN

"PLEASE," I BEGGED. "You are the only one I can talk to."

"I doubt I can be of any more service to you, milady."

He was probably right. I searched for something he might know, any question that might keep him with me. "What sort of traps await me?"

Eli turned away and ran his fingers through his hair, then faced me again. "Pits so deep that a werewolf could not claw his way out, giant iron jaws that clamp shut and could sever a foot, and nets too strong to break and too fine to slip through."

But a shifter could change into a bird and be free of all the traps. I took a deep breath and exhaled, stalling so he might stay longer. "How many shape-shifters are in the castle?"

"Only my sister Isabella and myself."

This was not good news. "Are you sure there are not others here like you?"

He inclined his head. "Positive."

I spun around so he could not see my face. Eli's declaration confirmed the shape-shifter in the king's chamber was indeed his sister. My throat thickened.

"Why does the king keep you?"

"My work is among the finest in the country. Possessing my weapons strengthens the king's army in battle." He lip curled into a sneer. "And I cost him very little to keep."

Searching the immediate vicinity, I spotted a log and sat. "You can turn into anything you wish?"

He shot me a sidelong glance. "How does learning about shape-shifters help you formulate your escape plan?"

"It does not." I lowered my gaze and softened my voice. "But it gives me insight into you."

He stared at me a long moment and I began to regret my honesty. "You should not be here, least of all with me."

"I am well aware of that." I folded my hands in my lap and looked into his eyes. "Yet I am still here."

Eli swallowed, then turned away. "We may turn into any animal we wish. The closer it is to our own weight, the easier to stay in that shape for lengthy periods."

"So, for instance, you could not stay as a rat for very long?" I asked, thinking of his sister.

"A few hours at the most, then I would need to return to my human form."

"And if you were unable to?" I pressed my lips together.

"It would be torture and I would become weaker." He tilted his head. "Thinking of ways to make me suffer?"

"If I wanted to inflict pain upon you, I need only to whisper in the ear of my future husband." I rolled my eyes and after a moment, continued. "Would it be easier to turn into an overly large rat?"

He lifted one brow. "What is this obsession with vermin?"

"Humor me." I forced a smile, wondering if I should tell him about the rat in the king's chamber.

"Size does not make it easier in that case, since two-hundred-pound rats do not occur in nature." He faced me again. "We can squeeze our weight into something smaller, but we have to change back sooner. If we shift into something which approximates our own weight, in theory, we could stay in the shape forever." Eli's eyes darkened. "But being human is much of what we are and if we stray from that too long, we will become weaker."

Eli could shift into a small animal, then sneak into the room, change into his human from and free his sister. But if she was quite weak, how would he get her out without endangering them both? He certainly could not leave the king's chambers in his human form. How else would he carry her out?

"How long have you and your sister been here?"

"My sister was sixteen when she was brought here. I was eighteen." His jaw tensed. "That was three years ago."

"Are you able to speak with her through thoughts?"

"We used to, but we've not been able to do that for some time." He shook his head and shoved a hand into his pocket. "She is too weak now."

"When she was stronger, she did not tell you where

they kept her?" I asked.

"She did not know. When they moved her, they covered the cage and she was unable to see her surroundings. I spent many evenings in other forms searching the castle."

"But you believe her to be alive?" I studied him, his faith and loyalty overwhelming me.

"I occasionally ask the king a question only she can answer. Something to do with our childhood or secrets we told each other. She lives."

Which I already knew. I desperately wanted to sneak into the king's room and free her—if she was still there and had not been moved. But even if I succeeded, once the king discovered her missing, he and his guards would search the castle and grounds. Since Isabella was so frail, she would slow Eli down and they might both get killed. And it would be my fault. When the king caught my scent, he would know I was the one who took her.

There had to be another way. I pondered it and let the silence linger as I glanced up at the stars.

"Since she is too weak to answer the king with her thoughts, he must allow her to be human again, at least long enough to provide the answer he needs." He drew in a deep breath. "Sometimes I fear I shall run out of questions for her, then he will kill her and I shall never know."

"I envy you to have that kind of love in your life." I lowered my head as tears burned my eyes. I cleared my throat, needing to change the subject. I could not think about the love he had for his sister and her fate. Or Eli's. "Why are there no guards here in the woods?"

"They watch farther out, on the other side of the forest. Now and then, someone from the king's court will roam these woods. Sometimes even the king himself. The king feels it is impractical to waste his resources watching those who have no desire to leave. But if they find anyone out there," Eli jerked his head toward the unfamiliar part of the forest, "they assume he is a rogue."

I nodded, unable to get his sister off my mind. "Where is the rest of your family?"

"I have not seen them since I was ten." His lip curled in disgust. "Shape-shifters are prone to vanishing when werewolves are around."

And I was one of *them*.

We lapsed into silence again. I wanted to stay but I knew I could not. I pushed myself off the boulder and straightened my shoulders. "I must go." But neither of us moved as we watched each other. I offered a small smile. "Thank you for the conversation."

"Meet me here tomorrow and I will teach you how to shoot the bow."

Though I craved his company, I wanted him to know I was not completely helpless. I lifted my chin. "I am already proficient."

His brows rose. "And how, pray tell, did you manage to learn? Surely, the men in your village did not allow this."

"No, they did not. My mother sent me out to pick

wildflowers and I snuck away with my father's bow. I learned enough."

The corners of his mouth lifted. "After tomorrow, you will be even better. Bring that sword, and I shall teach you how to use it as well."

"Thank you." So he had known all along that I had stolen his sword. And he had still come to meet me tonight. My insides warmed and I gave him a shy smile. "Until tomorrow."

At full speed, I rushed toward the granary and slipped into the tunnels. At the bottom of the stairs, I took my first step down the corridor and a rat rustled at the hem of my robe. A common gray rat. Those same rats were all over the castle and its grounds.

Something tugged on a memory and a vision of the king's chamber swam before me. The rat in her cage looked like the one I had just seen. If they appeared the same, could I replace Isabella with a common rat?

My stomach sank. No, of course not. The king would immediately sense the new rat was not a shape-shifter as easily as I had sensed that it was. He would know at once he had been betrayed. Everyone would be watched more closely and I would never escape. Even if he never noticed the shape-shifter had been replaced, I would leave my scent and he would know I had been in his room.

Saving Isabella was impossible. Eli would never leave and he would be a slave forever. I could not save either of them. My throat burned in frustration.

† † †

After breakfast the next morning, the king and I strolled arm-in-arm outside the castle. Guards kept close, which afforded us little privacy. For that, I was grateful.

In the distance, a crowd gathered to watch a game of shinty. I had zero interest in watching a bunch of men hitting a leather-wrapped ball back and forth across a field. When the prince joined us and we began to move toward the spectators, I realized I had little choice in the matter.

As we watched the game, King Mortimer slid his arm around my shoulder. I clenched my jaw and forced myself not to flinch as his fingertips made little circles on the fabric of my dress.

Just a few more days and he would leave for two whole weeks.

Suddenly, he spun around, his gaze dropping to my mouth. "I want some time to get to know you before our wedding."

I blinked, uncertain what he meant by that. We were spending time together now. How was it not sufficient? I prayed he did not expect me in his bed.

The sound of chainmail clanged as one of his guards bowed before us. "Your Majesty, I must speak with you regarding a pressing matter."

Struggling to conceal my urgent need to get away from the king, I smiled. "Would you excuse me a moment? I must see Mrs. Benton regarding my wedding gown."

"Of course, my dear." He leaned forward to brush his lips against my cheek then straightened and winked. "I will see you tonight," he whispered for my ears only.

My stomach churned at the implication. As soon as I turned, I located Mrs. Benton and began making my way. Feeling myself begin to speed up, I forced myself to slow my pace so I would not appear too eager.

I would definitely be retiring early to my chamber. If the king tried to visit me there, I would most certainly pretend to be fast asleep. I prayed that would be enough to deter him.

CHAPTER EIGHT

THAT EVENING, THE servants helped me with my bath. While they brushed out my hair, I commented on my fatigued state, hoping the king would overhear. When they left, I made sure the adjoining door was locked, then crawled under the covers.

A few minutes later, King Mortimer tapped lightly on our door and I concentrated on breathing deeply and steadily, as though I were asleep. Moments later, his footsteps receded and I relaxed. No doubt, the mysterious woman would visit him in his chambers shortly and I would be forgotten. But if the king decided to unlock my door and sneak into my room before she arrived, I could not be missing. I waited until I heard his other door open and shut, then feminine giggling, before being sure he would not pay me a late night visit.

After slipping into the tunnels, I stopped by his room and heard the woman's voice. They were both laughing. When the night's entertainment was over, very likely he would have little use for me. I shivered in relief.

Perhaps Isabella had been removed from his chambers. If she was still in his room, I would not envy her for being witness to everything going on with the king and his mistress. I grimaced at the idea as I made my way to the granary and then out the window toward the woods. When I slowed from my sprint, I did not have to search for Eli. I could smell his sweet, woodsy scent—so unlike the earthy scent of a werewolf. He was already waiting for me.

He stepped out from behind a tree, his blond hair tousled from the day and his shirt stained from the hours working with metals.

To me, he had never looked more handsome.

"Being here and helping you is dangerous. I mustn't stay long." He scanned the woods. "The king has ordered new swords for his journey and I have only a few days to make them."

I eyed the bow on the ground beside him. "I am sorry to keep you from your work."

"I have taken it upon myself to prepare you so that you may survive." He shrugged, then a wistful smile curved his mouth. "I long to see the king's face when his guards are unable to bring you back."

We both knew the king's guards never failed and the chance of surviving more than a matter of days was slim, but I did not correct him. At the very least, I hoped to be a source of great frustration to the werewolves as they tried to capture me. "Then we should get started."

"We can use this one." He bent over and snatched

the bow near his feet, then strode toward the clearing. "I have already set up targets for practice."

He stopped at a fallen tree and swiveled to face me. "I shall like to see your form first." Eli handed me the bow, then pointed to a tree branch with a red ribbon. "Go ahead."

Facing the target, I positioned the arrow against the curve of the bow, then raised it.

"Aim with your shoulder." Eli moved behind me and nudged me until I stood sideways, my shoulder pointing at the branch.

My skin tingled where he had touched me and my stomach fluttered.

"Raise the bow and pull the arrow, but do not release it yet."

I glanced over my shoulder, but turned away when I realized how close we were. Close enough that his scent wafted up my nose, making me dizzy. My right arm trembled and I lowered the bow.

"Are you okay?" His breath tickled my neck and sent chills over my skin.

"Yes, but a demonstration might be helpful." And it would allow for some much needed distance from him, so I could think again.

Eli stepped back, taking his heady scent with him, and my limbs steadied. He took the bow from me, aimed his shoulder toward the red ribbon and demonstrated each action as he spoke. "When you are ready, raise the bow, nock the arrow, pull. Keep your elbow high."

His fingers gradually straightened and the arrow shot dead center in the branch. He turned to me and relinquished the bow. I accepted it and grabbed another arrow from the quiver. Raising the bow, I positioned the arrow, then pulled.

"Three fingers." Eli moved behind me and, with one hand over mine, he kept the bow still. He reached around my other side and his chest brushed my shoulder, sending a tingle down my arms. His fingertips grazed the back of my hand and my breath caught.

I needed to concentrate on the task at hand, not fall for a shape-shifter I could never be with.

"Touch your thumb and pinky together so they stay out of the way. Use the other three to pull." He tapped under my arm. "Elbow up. Pull, aim and shoot."

I looked down the arrow, pulled a little more, then let the arrow fly. It grazed the side of the branch.

"Well done." Eli grinned. "Again. This time, make your motions fluid. Nock the arrow, raise the bow, pull, aim and fire. Your best chance of hitting your target is within the first few seconds, before your muscles begin to lose focus."

Counting in my head, I raised, pulled, aimed and released. I did not hit the center, but the arrow had been closer this time.

Eli chuckled. "You are a natural."

"I have an excellent teacher." I grinned, but it slowly faded as I held his gaze. I wondered how our lives would have been different had he not been a slave and I not a prisoner promised to the king.

If shape-shifters were accepted as equals, would we have stood a chance, maybe fallen in love and perhaps one day marry?

He took a step toward me and gently took the bow from my grasp. He leaned over to set it on the ground, moving closer in the process. His eyes dropped to my mouth and I held my breath. Every cell in my body screamed for him to kiss me.

Shaking it off, he pushed backward and cleared his throat as he threaded his fingers through his hair. "You can practice with the bow after I leave. Now I want to see how you use a blade. Mind you, the sound will carry farther than our voices or the arrows. We must take care. Did you bring the stolen sword?"

Obviously, he had not inspected my hiding place or he would not have asked.

"Yes." I quickly located the spot, retrieved the sword and scabbard, then held out the handle for him to take.

"Not my finest work." Eli examined the narrow blade and minimal hilt, then pulled a sword from near the tree where he had set the bow. The cross guard was longer than any I had seen before, the blade slightly wider. "This one promises to endure long past your opponent's."

"It is beautiful," I said, running my thumb along the razor-sharp edge.

"You must take this one instead."

My eyes snapped to his. "The king will not miss it?"

One side of his mouth curved up. "He cannot miss what he has no knowledge of."

I returned his smile. "I have spent less time with swords than bows. I am not very good."

Eli picked up the other sword and held it ready. "Then we shall practice."

† † †

I saw little of King Mortimer the next day, except during meals. Apparently, I had been presented, shown off and was no longer needed. The wedding plans and standing for the dressmaker kept me busy, though it was a terrible waste of time. I planned to be gone long before I would need it.

After supper, the king sat with the prince while the minstrels played music. Some of the court stayed, as did Mrs. Benton who sat with me. She prattled on, as though she had become feeble with age, flitting from one subject to the next. But I knew her wit was still sharper than ever when she skillfully sprinkled in details I might need to escape.

Mrs. Benton chattered on about a pig that had escaped a few weeks ago and how the guards on the north side of the castle had spotted it from the tower. She went on to tell me how the guards who held post on the other side of the woods had once caught a shape-shifter trying to infiltrate the castle as a common house cat. How I loved dear Mrs. Benton.

As I was laying down a card, a shadow fell over me and my shoulders tensed. I peered at Mrs. Benton and realized the king was speaking to her with his thoughts.

She rose from her chair. "Forgive me, milady, but I must attend to a matter immediately. May we continue this game another time?"

I gave her a polite smile, knowing the king gave her no choice but to leave. "Of course."

As King Mortimer lowered to her chair, I caught the scent of rancid pork in his beard, and shuddered.

He leaned back, his gaze sweeping over my waist and back up to my chest before one side of his mouth curled up. "You are looking exceedingly handsome this evening, my dear Hannah."

I mentally flinched, hoping he would leave it at that. "Thank you, Your Majesty. I am honored."

He crossed a leg over his knee and I squirmed under his gaze a long moment before he finally broke the silence. "Some packs prefer to follow human law, but we are not bound by the same moral codes."

I willed myself to keep from bolting and forced myself to smile. "Many human laws are useful in keeping peace among werewolves and humans alike. Surely, Your Majesty does not expect his court to behave in a manner that would bring shame into his home."

"But many of their rules do not apply to us." His eyes darted away for a split second before he lowered his voice. "For instance, female werewolves have no need to worry about bearing unwanted children since they are incapable of reproducing. You can rest easy knowing there are no repercussions to your indiscretions."

His meaning could not have been clearer and I could avoid the subject no longer. Revulsion rose up in my throat as I pinned him with a stare. "I am sure there are plenty of ladies who do not consider themselves worth waiting for, but I am not one of them."

His eyes narrowed and his jaw tightened. "Of course." Without another word, he rose, his robes whipping through the air.

My hands trembled in both relief and fear. I had gotten out of it this time, but at what price? If he made another advance and I were to reject him again... King Mortimer expected to get his way and when he did not, those to blame fell into disfavor. For now, I was still alive, but I might not be so lucky next time.

CHAPTER NINE

THAT NIGHT, I read a book by candlelight until the voices in the castle died down. When the king's mistress arrived at his chamber earlier than usual, I slipped out of my room and into the tunnel before running at full speed toward the woods. When I entered the forest clearing, Eli was already waiting for me. At the sight of his face, for an instant, I forgot about my dreadful day with the king, and that if I did not act soon, I might be forced into his bed.

Eli offered me a warm, generous smile then bowed. "Milady."

I inclined my head and returned his smile. "You came."

"I am a man of my word." His smile faded. "However, I question the prudence of our meeting. I worry not for myself, as I am far too useful for the king to discard. He will punish me, then put me back to work. You... you may not fare so well."

"Yes." I dropped my gaze and sighed. "It seems my choices all lead to one destiny. If the outcome is the same, does it really matter how I get there?"

"I suppose not." He leaned over to gather some arrows. "I made more for you."

My stomach dipped as he offered me a quiver full of arrows. He may as well have presented me with a vase full of wildflowers.

But I was putting far too much importance on a simple act of kindness. I needed arrows to shoot and, being a practical sort, he made them for me. That was all there was to it. "Thank you. I appreciate all you have done. I only wish I could return your kindness."

"Learn, escape and stay alive. That is how you shall repay me."

A less generous person would have pleaded with me to help him find and free his sister. But Eli asked only for my safety. His selflessness made me admire him even more.

After over an hour of practice, Eli rose from his spot on a stone. "My apologies, milady, but I must take my leave soon."

"Yes, of course." I slipped an arrow back into the quiver and darted toward the ribboned branch to re-claim the other arrows.

He moved to stand beside me. As I reached over to retrieve an arrow, so did Eli and his hand covered mine. I froze when his hand did not move, except for his thumb that slid across my knuckle.

My gaze met his.

He yanked his hand away, shaking his head. "I beg your forgiveness."

"You do not require my forgiveness, nor shall I offer it." Slowly, I tugged on his hand, bringing his palm to my cheek and holding my breath, afraid he would leave.

Eli took a cautious step forward, his eyes trained on me. His hand slipped behind my neck and he pulled me toward him until his forehead touched mine. "I am afraid I have grown much too fond of you," he whispered.

I gripped his sleeve and inched closer. Just a little farther and my lips would touch his.

He stepped away and blew out a breath. "We must keep our distance. You cannot risk anyone catching shape-shifter scent on you."

I spun away and squeezed my eyes shut. Not only would I soon be far, far from Eli, but I had to take care how much I enjoyed his company during my last days with him. I sighed. "I have stayed too long and you have work to do."

Eli nodded. "Tomorrow then?"

I smiled wistfully. "Yes."

† † †

The prince left the following morning. King Mortimer spent the majority of the next few days in his study or meeting with his advisors. I enjoyed the sunshine, taking long walks each day or going for a ride. And every night, I met Eli. He helped me with sword fighting maneuvers and improving the aim of my arrows. We shared conversation and smiles, but he took care to always keep his distance.

Much to my relief, I barely saw King Mortimer as he prepared for his trip. Finally, he departed with much fanfare, promising to return in two weeks. I vowed to be gone long before then.

During the day while he worked, Eli had listened in on every conversation possible and learned that the king would travel over two hundred miles throughout his two-week trip. But one could cover only so many miles a day by horse. If I tried to leave tonight, King Mortimer very likely would not be more than a few miles away. After tomorrow, there may be only fifty miles between us. If I waited another day, he could be a hundred miles away and would take longer getting back once news of my escape reached him. This would give me a better head start, in addition to increasing the odds of my trail being harder to follow.

Just two more days with Eli. I would make the most of it.

That evening as I stepped into the clearing, my heart pounded in my chest. From his seat on a fallen log, Eli trained his eyes on me and for a few moments neither of us spoke.

I took a seat about two feet away on the large boulder. "Two evenings from now, I shall leave."

He nodded. "I will be sorry to see you go. I have enjoyed our conversations."

"As have I." Feeling shy, I glanced away.

"I... I have not asked before, because I cannot allow you to put yourself in danger on my behalf or my sister's, but... if there was a way you could find out where she is being held, without risking your position..."

It had been days since I saw the caged rat. I did not even know for sure if that was Isabella or if the king had acquired another shifter without Eli's knowledge. Even if I could be certain, I had no idea if the king had moved her. If Eli broke into the king's private suite, his efforts could all be for nothing. And he would leave his scent behind. The king would know Eli had been in his room and he would be punished — possibly killed — for having been there.

Unless I was absolutely positive of Isabella's location, I could not give him any information at all. Still, guilt overwhelmed me. If I were in his position, I would probably give anything to hear news of my loved one. "If I discover her whereabouts, I shall tell you."

We sparred hard for over an hour before we took a break. Panting from exertion, my hands raw and aching, I had never been more grateful for werewolves' quick healing. If I were human, anyone would look at my hands and know what I had been up to. I climbed back onto the big rock to rest as my breathing leveled. Eli maintained his distance, as he always did, by leaning against a tree at least two yards away.

"I daresay your skills at battle are much improved."

"You are too kind." I shot him a smile. "It is exaggeration, I am sure, but I hope it will be enough since we have only one more day to practice."

In an instant, he stood in front of me. "I implore you to reconsider. Fall at His Majesty's feet and beg his mercy. Anything so that you may live."

"Being with a man I detest is not living." I shook my head and laughed dryly. "And we both know his mind is set."

"You can make him love you. Do whatever it takes. Surely, being his queen cannot be so terrible. And after ruling a couple centuries, he is certainly well-respected."

"He is not respected by me." I rose from the rock and scowled. "I could never be with him."

"You cannot know that." He visibly stiffened. "Given time, you might grow to love him."

"To love anyone else," I lowered my voice to a whisper, since that was all I could manage, "became impossible the moment I met you." My muscles tensed and my stomach dipped as I awaited his reaction to my confession.

Eli took a step forward and closed the distance as he searched my face. "You mustn't say such things. It will only get you killed."

"Indeed, it may. But leaving the castle could also get me killed. Surely, staying will get me killed. Why should I care since the outcome is the same?"

I only had to reach out to touch him. I wanted to. But would he push me away? I could not stand to be rejected by the man I loved.

His jaw tightened and he stared at me for a long moment. "Because I am selfish. For every day you live, I can keep breathing." His tone softened. "You are the only thing that makes this place tolerable. Yet somehow, seeing you every day, and not being able to touch you, is almost unbearable."

My breath caught in my throat. After that confession, rejection and impropriety were the last things on my mind. I reached for his hand and tugged, pulling him closer. He shook his head, but his eyes never left mine as I snaked my arms around his neck and melted against him.

"This is a mistake," Eli whispered as he brushed a lock of hair off my face and cupped my cheek. "The worst decision we could possibly make." He closed his eyes before slowly leaning in.

My limbs trembled and my pulse raced as I waited for him to kiss me. Then his lips gently brushed mine and fire exploded through my middle and blazed to my hands and toes. He wrapped his arms all the way around me, one hand cradling my head, the other pressing me closer against him. I moaned and my lips parted.

Then suddenly, he whipped backward and landed several yards away. "We cannot risk it. My scent will be all over you and yours on me."

I nodded, knowing I needed to leave him before I got us both killed. "I will be back tomorrow." Without waiting for a reply, I spun and headed back to the castle. My pace slowed as I entered the tunnel, my spirits weary from Eli's absence. Pausing, I leaned against the cold stone and squeezed my eyes shut. How could I leave Eli now that I loved him? But knowing that the king planned to murder me, how could I stay?

I took a deep breath and opened my eyes. My gaze landed on a shadow where the stone wall met the floor in front of me. A dead rat. I turned toward my chambers then stopped, thinking of Eli's sister. Had she escaped?

Of course not. Common gray rats were everywhere. And they were usually just rats. However, since the animal was dead, I would never know if it was a real rat or a shifter. Once werewolves or shifters were in their animal form, unless they were abnormally large, no one could tell if it had once been human or always been a rat.

I prayed it was not Isabella. She was probably still in the king's room and he would never allow the possibility of escape.

Wait... since no one could tell that this rat had never been a shifter, it could take the place of Isabella and the king would never know it was not her.

I shivered knowing I would have to touch the dead thing. I reached down and, with its tail pinched between my fingers, took a deep breath and headed for my room. In the candlelight, I inspected it again. I could not imagine anyone noticing it was a different rat. They would assume Isabella had died and no one would look for her. She would reunite with Eli and they would both be free.

My chest squeezed at the thought of losing Eli. But at least he and his sister would be safe. That was all that mattered.

But first, I had to make the switch.

My heart pounded as I checked for a presence in the room next door. Hearing nothing, I tried the knob and the door opened. I made my way toward the rat cage and my limbs trembled.

Isabella, I am a friend of Eli's. I shall free you but I

need you to remain very quiet. I already knew she was incapable of answering me, but I prayed she understood. *I also need you to stay in your rat form or we may get caught.*

The cage locked from the outside, but did not require a key. I simply flipped the latch and opened the door. Reaching in, I lay my palm up and waited, but she did not approach me. *As soon as I have you, I will leave a dead rat in your stead. No one will come looking for you.*

A moment later, her tiny paws tickled my palm. I withdrew my hand from the cage and carefully slipped her into my pocket. *Please do not move.* I reached into my other pocket to retrieve the dead rat and placed it in the cage.

I closed the cage door and turned, intending to rush out, but my gaze caught on a bag sitting on the king's bureau. It looked like the same bag filled with gold coins I had noticed the other night, though now it was closed. I tiptoed across the room and my heart beat wildly as I reached my hand inside and grabbed a generous serving of the gold coins. I hurried back to my room and locked the door.

I concentrated, directing my thoughts to Eli. *It is imperative you meet me at our spot. Now.*

CHAPTER TEN

WITH ISABELLA IN her rat form tucked safely in the pocket of my robe, I ducked back into the tunnel and raced through the castle walls. Moments later, I stood in the woods, my pulse pounding at my temple.

I had just finished stowing the coins in my hiding place, inside the quiver, when a twig snapped. I whirled around. At the sight of Eli, my eyes misted.

"Hannah, what is it?" He grasped my shoulders. "What has happened?"

"I have something to show you." I swallowed and reached into my pocket. Grabbing his other hand, I gently placed the rat on his palm.

"A rat?" An instant later, he inhaled sharply, his eyes wide as they searched mine. "Isabella? How —"

"Do not concern yourself with how, only that soon everyone will believe her to be dead." I watched him stroke Isabella's furry spine.

"Then she is free to turn human." Eli kneeled and lowered Isabella to the moist dirt.

The tiny form shivered and quivered until it became a blur, then disappeared. In a flash, a young woman sat on the ground before me. Isabella was blond like Eli and about my height but with a willowy build. She moved to get up, then staggered back.

Eli wrapped his arms around her and pulled her up.

"I thought I would never see you again." She croaked as she grabbed a handful of his shirt, her white nightdress rustling in the breeze through her muffled sobs.

He stroked her hair. "You are safe. He will never hurt you again."

Not wanting to intrude, I slowly backed away.

He glanced over his sister's shoulder, his gaze landing on me. "Do not go."

"She is free now and so are you. You can... leave." My throat swelled at the thought of being without Eli.

"I do not know how to thank you." Isabella stepped out of Eli's embrace, wobbled to me and dropped to her knees. "I am indebted."

I gave a nervous laugh. "Hardly. Your brother paid that debt ahead of time. You owe me nothing."

Eli shook his head. "We will stay until it is time for you to leave."

"But I must wait until the king is farther away and it is too dangerous for you to stay." I waved my arms for Isabella to get off her knees and she rose shakily. "You must not delay and risk losing more than just your freedom."

"Once I escape, the guards will be on high alert and you may lose your chance forever." He shook his head. "And Isabella needs to regain her strength. She and I will wait and see you to safety, then —"

"Part ways?" I choked on the question and released Isabella. "Risk everything that way, then forget we ever knew each other?"

He wrapped an arm around Isabella's waist and she leaned into him. "I will do everything in my power to ensure you find a haven. Once you are there, we *must* separate. Traveling with a fugitive slave will be far more dangerous for you than running on your own. We are different species. We will be noticed everywhere we go."

I wanted Eli and Isabella to leave immediately, but if they refused and we ran together, I saw no point in separating once we were out of harm's way. I wanted him with me forever. "Is that your preference? Because I am quite certain that since I met you, I have developed an aversion to being without you."

"Hannah, be reasonable." He ran his free hand through his hair. "Do not make this more difficult than it needs to be."

As if realizing there was more going on between us than she had originally thought, Isabella moved to back away, but he held tight to her slender frame as if unwilling to let her go so soon.

"Because you do not wish to be with me?" Could I have misjudged his feelings for me so completely?

"I am a shape-shifter who will always be a peasant. I am weaker than you, scorned by your kind." He growled. "Your people will hunt me simply because I dared to take what was not mine. You will be in enough danger once you escape without adding my problems. You will be safer without me."

"My heart will be safer *with* you." I let that hang in the air as I watched emotions wash over his face—confusion, anger. And something else... hope. "I love you, Eli."

He exhaled, then lifted Isabella, carried her to the boulder and carefully sat her on it. Eli turned toward me, a pained look on his face. I did not see him move again, only felt his warm hands the next moment around my waist as they pulled me close. He dropped his forehead on my shoulder. *As you wish. I will run with you for all eternity, if that is what we must to do.*

My eyes pooled as I cupped his face and pulled him toward me. His lips touched mine and I knew everything would be all right. So long as I had him by my side.

But before we could truly be together, we had to escape the castle. In just hours from now, we would leave and I still no plan. I had wanted Eli since the moment I had laid eyes on him. But as much as I loved him, I knew I would get him killed. He and Isabella could change into birds and fly. The king and his guards could not track their scent. I, on the other hand, had to travel by foot. Wherever I ran, they would follow. It was only a matter of time before the werewolves caught up and killed us all.

I had known since the beginning that my chances of dying were strong. But Eli could easily avoid the werewolves undetected. If he was discovered and murdered, it would be because of me.

Eli and I could never be together.

I went limp in his arms, my eyes stinging with tears. "But how am I to get past the guards and traps? We both know I cannot do what you can. I could not bear to watch you risk your life by staying with me when you could —"

He held my face and stared into my eyes. "We have two days to find a way. Together."

Eli was determined, but was that enough? With his help and Isabella's, could I survive the danger awaiting me?

"Why wait?" Isabella asked. "The three of us should leave tonight while we are able to."

Eli released me and focused on his sister. "You can barely stand. You need to eat and rest to get your strength back. We mustn't risk getting caught because you are too weak."

"After a meal, I will heal enough to travel. If we fly, we leave no trail to follow. Once we are a few miles away, we can stop and I can finish healing."

I squeezed my eyes shut, not wanting to give Eli an option to leave me. But I had to, because I needed him to survive. "Isabella is right. She can do it and you are strong enough to help her. I, on the other hand, will only hold you back."

"I will not leave you behind." His jaw set as he shook his head.

"But you must. I... I should have told you this be-fore..." I sucked in a lungful of air, my eyes burning as I met Eli's gaze. "King Mortimer wants to start a war with your species. He intends to murder me and blame my death on *you*. He needs you here in order to accomplish that. Surely you do not think that his only means of keeping you here—Isabella—is not foremost in his mind. He would be a fool to leave without making sure his servants feed her, and instructing his guards to inform him immediately if anything happens."

Eli's eyes hardened. "This changes nothing."

I sighed. "The farther away the king gets, the longer it will take him to return and the more time I will have to make sure I am well ahead of him. Right now, he is probably close by. If I escape and he is alerted straight away, he could be here tomorrow and I will be too easy to track and catch. I must wait until he has had the chance to cover more miles. And even that will not guarantee a successful escape. You, on the other hand, may leave any time you wish and he will never find you. If you wait with me, anything could happen and we may all die."

"I, too, refuse to leave this place without you," Isabella added. "You gave me my life back. Let us give you yours."

They were making a huge mistake. What if the king was alerted immediately of the rat's death and returned straightaway? My only hope was to believe that the death of a shape-shifter was of little consequence to him and was not worth adjusting his plans. "You must realize that if he suspects we are together, he will never stop until he finds us."

Isabella nodded confidently, glancing over at her brother. "Then we will never stop running."

Eli leaned into me, and laid his palms on my cheeks. "Together."

CHAPTER ELEVEN

THE NEXT MORNING, shouts from the king's room woke me. His steward had discovered the dead rat and someone was being dispatched immediately to inform King Mortimer. I had hoped the dead rat would go unnoticed, which would buy me time before the king was notified.

I had not expected to leave until the next evening, but now I needed to speed up my plan. The king could decide that a dead rat was not worth sacrificing the opportunity to intimidate the people of his kingdom. On the other hand, he may want to tend to the matter immediately. Waiting another day would be foolish, because he could already be back before I had a chance to leave.

Shortly after nightfall later that evening, I would retire to my room and when the castle settled, I would sneak out. By the time anyone missed me at mass the next morning, I would be long gone. I fervently hoped the king was not close enough to hear telepathically and that the rider would have great difficulty locating him. More than likely, that was not to be.

Eli, they have discovered the rat and are already on their way to find King Mortimer, I told him from my room. *We must leave tonight.*

Let me know when you are ready and we shall meet in the woods.

And do what? I still had no idea how Eli and Isabella could travel with me by ground without being tracked. My stomach knotted. I wondered how she was doing. I hoped Eli had managed to bring her enough food so she could rebuild her strength.

With no obligation to spend my day with the king, I sought out Mrs. Benton, the only werewolf I would miss when I left. From her overstuffed chair, she laid a card faceup.

I grinned. "You beat me again."

She raised a brow, her mouth curving up. "You are in awfully good spirits about it today."

"I want to enjoy my time with you." I lifted a shoulder.

Her smile faded. *You will be leaving soon.* When I offered no reply, she rose and gathered me in an embrace. *You are not one who would be easily caged. For your peace of mind, you must be free. I understand this. But I do so wish you could be content with everything the king has to offer.*

If Mrs. Benton only knew of the king's plan to kill me, she would not be so quick to urge me to stay. *Unfortunately, I cannot be content as a prisoner. But I will think of you often, dear Mrs. Benton.*

And I will miss you, child. I only hope you have found a way to do the impossible. Be safe. Her mouth trembled against my shoulder and I squeezed her tighter.

That evening, I retired to my chamber and sprawled out on my bed. Though I did not intend to fall asleep, I needed to rest up for my escape—which I still had not planned. How would I get past the guards and evade the traps?

I could only think to avoid other parts of the forest where werewolves might lurk. Perhaps stay out in the open where I could see what lay ahead. Other than that, I would rely on luck. I would run, finding rivers and streams to wash away my scent, until the trackers lost me. And then I would keep running.

One thing I knew for certain: if I were still here by morning, I could be trapped at the castle until the king murdered me.

Thinking of what he intended to do made me shiver as I locked the door, as well as the one adjoining the king's chamber. I returned to my bed and checked for the dagger I had placed under my pillow.

The bed was soft and my lids grew heavy. But I would not fall asleep. I needed to be awake after the castle occupants fell into slumber.

It seemed like mere moments had passed when I bolted upright. Though I had not been fully asleep, I had relaxed enough to let my mind wander and lose sense of time.

A large shadow fell in front of the door to the king's room and sweat beaded at my temples. My vision adjusted to the pitch-dark of night, but the shadow was gone. Assuming my tired eyes were playing tricks on me, I fell back against the pillow in relief, air whooshing from my lungs.

I blinked as I became more alert. Someone was in my room.

My heart thumped erratically as I lay there, unsure what to do. Why had he come back so soon? I did not even want to imagine why he would be in my room. I slowly stretched up to a sitting position. "Your Majesty, you startled me."

He stalked closer until he was looming over me. "I cannot imagine why it would come as a surprise that your future husband would be in your bedroom."

I forced my breathing to slow and my heart to beat slower, though revulsion ruled as it crawled up my spine. How could he be back so soon? And how would I escape now that the king and all his men were back? I could not allow him to see my fear, nor did I want him to think I would let him take me before the wedding.

One thing at a time. First, I needed to get him out of my room. "I am surprised because I did not expect you back so soon. In any case, you are not my husband *yet*. Does milord want to rush the ceremony?"

He lowered to the side of my bed and leaned over to stroke my face. "Such beauty should not be wasted one more day. Whether we marry tomorrow or in one month, you belong to me."

I forced myself still so I would not cringe at his touch. "I thought you planned to be gone at least another week. Did something happen? Is everyone all right?"

"My party is fine. But during dinner, I received a messenger who delivered unfortunate news. Other than that, all is well."

I swallowed, wondering what the unfortunate news was. Death of his shape-shifter prisoner perhaps? But how did he get here so fast? "During dinner? You could not have been very far away."

"Just a few miles. I wanted to stay close."

If only I had anticipated that, I would have left earlier. "I hope the news was not too distressing."

He shrugged. "Yes and no. It requires me to adjust my plans."

Altering his plans for *me*? This could not be good. "I must wonder, then, what news would be so terrible that you would risk your good name by coming to my bed before we are married."

"I do not follow human rules. In any case, 'tis no risk at all since no one knows I am here." His hand traveled up from my waist, over my breast and then moved against my throat. "I left the duke's manor nearby without anyone knowing. I will be back before sunup, before anyone is aware I was ever gone."

Which will give him an alibi after his future wife turns up dead.

He lowered his mouth to mine and kissed me hard, his tongue forcing my mouth open as he moved his full weight on top of me. My legs were trapped under my skirt and completely useless in aiding me in defense.

So that he would not suspect anything, I moaned to show my pleasure while my other hand stroked his back. Tears welled in my eyes as I slid my arm under my pillow to reach for the dagger.

In one swift move, I thrust the knife into his side, shoved him off me and lunged toward the window. But that would not delay him for more than a moment. He was quite strong and healed too quickly. I could attempt to cut off his head, but he would kill me long before I could accomplish it.

My only choice was to run.

Pulse racing, I leaped up onto the sill, opened the window and jumped. Just as I hit the air, his hand wrapped around my ankle and I plummeted, my shoulder smashing into the castle wall.

I hung there, upside down by my ankle, my shoulder throbbing. There were no witnesses, no one roaming about the grounds. The king had only to pull me up and back into my chambers, cut off my head with my own dagger and leave. No one would know what he did. Eli would be blamed and the king would have his war.

Eli... He might already be waiting for me in the woods and wondering where I was, maybe even contemplating putting himself at risk to look for me. Or worse, he might still be working on swords by lantern and easy to find when the angry werewolves came to punish him for murdering the king's beloved.

CHAPTER TWELVE

KING MORTIMER SQUEEZED my ankles and I winced. Still upside-down, I clawed at the stone on the outside of the castle wall, trying to gain purchase, but to no avail. I was as helpless as Isabella had been before I had freed her.

Eli! I shouted silently to only him, since I did not want the king to know Eli had been alerted. *The king is here and he knows about Isabella. You must run immediately!*

Now that Eli had been warned, he and Isabella had a chance. Unlike me.

The king yanked me up by my ankles and dragged me back through the window. In that moment, I knew beyond any doubt that I was about to die.

But I would not make it easy for him.

He captured my hands, his gaze locking onto mine as he tossed me back onto the bed. In a flash, he was over me. "How did you know?"

"Know about what?" I squirmed beneath him.

"That I intended to end your life." He sneered.

Blood stained his shirt, but the dagger was gone. Where was it? "I had no knowledge of that. I just could not bear another second of your hands on me." I spit in his face. I was going to die anyway, right?

His fist came down on me, and my cheek cracked under the force. Tears welled in my eyes as he ripped the shoulder of my nightgown, his lips diving for my neck. He licked my skin and I shivered.

He froze. "You smell like shape-shifter. How is that possible?"

I met his eyes, glaring. "How else?"

The king glanced over his shoulder, his gaze falling on the dagger he had thrown to the foot of the bed. Pinning me down with one hand, he reached for the blade. His weight lifted just enough that I could move and I shoved my knee into his groin. He flinched and I grabbed the dagger from his hand. Lunging toward him, I kicked him in the face with all my werewolf strength. Blood splattered from his mouth as his head thrust backward.

This time, he reached out when I jumped through the window, but his fingers only brushed my heels as I plummeted toward the ground. I righted myself, my feet landing with a thud on the soft grass. I ran toward the woods to my stash of weapons.

The trees stood welcoming just a few yards away and I forced myself to run faster. Almost there...

Hands clamped onto my calves and I face-planted. The king flipped me over and straddled my waist, locking my arms over my head. He easily held my wrists with one hand while his other retrieved the dagger. "You have spirit, I grant you that. Such a shame to waste it all. You would have made a proper queen."

"If you kill me here, someone is bound to see." I raised my voice so anyone nearby could hear. He might succeed in killing me, but his plan to blame it on Eli would be ruined. "Like your guards at the battlement. Surely you do not think you can fool them into thinking it was someone else when they can see you now."

His face twisted in fury. "Enough!" He pressed the blade to my throat.

"Do it!" I shouted. "I will gratefully choose death over having your hands on me ever again."

He could not blame my death on the shifter, but I could see he no longer cared. The blade pierced my skin, burning my neck like fire. Slowly, he sliced back and forth, and I screamed inside my head as I squeezed my eyes shut against the agonizing pain. He could have already severed my neck, but his fury made him want to draw out my suffering. He had all the time in the world, because he was the king—no one would stop him.

Spots swam before my eyes and my lids shut as the king pushed on, and all feeling left my body. I lay there limp, waiting for death to find me.

An odd flapping noise sounded in the distance and an instant later, it grew loud enough to roar in my ears. Wind blew my long hair over my face and the king's shout followed a loud thump.

Then I was floating, my body hunched over. Why was I not flat on my back like I had been moments ago?

You will never be free, the king shouted into my head. *I will hunt you with my last breath, you and those lowly shifters. You will all pay for your treachery!*

"Everything will be all right," Eli shouted to be heard above the wind. "We have you."

But I could already feel myself slipping. He was too late.

† † †

Warmth spread through my fingers, like the sun after a rain. My eyes fluttered open to see two shapes before me.

"Hannah." Eli stroked a hand across my cheek.

"How are you feeling?" Isabella hovered over me.

"How…" My thoughts drifted. Had Eli and Isabella been found and killed, too? Was I in heaven? "Did they kill you, too?"

"You are safe, love," Eli said softly. "No one will find us here."

I tried to sit up, but Eli pressed a hand to my stomach. "Stay down. You need to heal."

I blinked, memories rushing me. "I thought he killed me."

"With just a little more time to sever your head, he may have succeeded," Isabella replied, lifting my head and holding a tin cup to my lips. "Here, drink this."

My lips parted and my body welcomed the cool liquid, but my throat rebelled in pain. I winced. "How did we get away?"

"We turned into eagles. Extremely large eagles." She took the cup away and set it aside. "We dove at the king and knocked him off you, then lifted you into the air. We flew away until we could no longer see the castle, then we changed direction. We are far, far away without leaving a trail for them to follow."

My lids drooped and their voices began to fade.

"Rest now, love. Heal." Eli brushed a moist cloth over my forehead. "We shall talk more when you are feeling better."

† † †

I woke on a soft bed, silk-like blankets against my skin. The sound of fabric rustling next to me beckoned me to turn my head.

"How are you feeling?" Isabella asked, rolling over on her side to face me.

I stretched, but stopped short at the ache in my neck and winced.

"Considering the damage, you are healing very well." She laid a gentle hand on my shoulder. "But you are still weak. Once you have eaten, you will heal even faster."

I nodded, grateful I had not died after all. "Where is Eli?" I croaked.

"Out hunting. I imagine he will be back soon." She sat up and reached over for a bowl at her bedside. "Are you hungry? I have soup and bread."

"Starving, thank you." I opened and she spooned soup into my mouth. I chewed and swallowed and almost instantly felt my body tingle as it repaired itself. "Where are we?"

"In a village about fifty miles north. You have been out for a whole day."

My eyes shot to hers. "An entire day? By now, everyone must know. The king probably has an army of guards searching for us. Fifty miles is not nearly far enough. We must go."

"We wanted to keep moving, but if we travel with you in that condition, any humans we encounter might ask too many questions. And so we waited."

"You should not have. You put yourselves in danger by staying with me. Very likely, the king's guards are already waiting in every city and port." My pulse raced. Any moment, the werewolves would explode into this village. "You must leave without me. I will only hold you back."

"If it were not for you, I would still be caged in the king's chamber." She patted my hand. "And if the king had followed through with his plan, I would soon be dead. The end of Eli's life would quickly follow. You saved our lives, Hannah. Please allow us to save yours."

"You already did. Your debt is paid." I bolted from the bed, groaning at the pain shooting through my neck, and glanced around for clothing. "You must not risk your lives for me anymore than you already have. Eli was right. It is much too dangerous for us to travel together."

"We saved *one* life. You saved *two*." She must have heard the footfalls right outside, because she rose from her spot on the bed. "You must at least allow us to see you to safety," she said before opening the door a few inches, swinging it open to reveal a young girl.

The girl curtsied, her arms full with what looked like a gown.

You have been asleep for a full day, Isabella told me silently. *I am afraid you must appear frail or they may wonder at your miraculous recovery.*

That would not be too difficult to manage since I did not have to pretend. I leaned against the wall and slouched. Wiping my brow, I gave the human a weak smile as I reached for the soup. The sooner I ate, the faster I would heal and we could leave.

"I have come to inquire about our patient," she said, stretching her arms toward Isabella. "And to give you these."

"I am much better, thank you," I answered. "Well enough to travel, I should think."

Isabella reached into her pocket and retrieved a gold coin. "Thank you for your fine gowns and shoes, but we will need two more. Can you accommodate us?"

The girl nodded.

"That is good news. How soon can the horses be ready?" Isabella asked.

"I will find out, milady." She bowed and backed out of the room.

I raised a brow. I barely knew Isabella, but already liked her. In another time and place, we could have been great friends. *Nicely done. How did you explain our situation?*

Isabella shrugged. *I had to provide an explanation as to why we arrived with no horses and improperly dressed—you in your torn nightgown and me with no*

*shoes, my brother in a tattered shirt and dirty breech-
es. I told them that our clothes were stolen as well as
the horses and our trunks. A gold coin from your quiver satisfied their curiosity well enough.*

I had all but forgotten about the gold I had taken
from the king's chambers, then stowed in the quiver.
I glanced around to make sure no one else was in the
room, then slipped out of my nightgown as I listened
to the low murmur of voices outside. I did not sense
any other werewolf or shifter nearby. "I hope you have
a plan for getting us away from the humans without
putting them in danger."

"Eli wanted to look around to make sure there
were no werewolves. Fortunately for us, our thoughts
cannot be heard this far. Even if he encounters a pack,
it is doubtful that word of our escape has reached this
distance. Do not worry. By the time any guards come
this way, our scent will be long gone."

I breathed a sigh of relief. Still, I could not get
out of this village and away from the humans soon
enough. *Eli, when will you return?*

I can see the village now. I will see you shortly.

The villagers' voices rose and I knew they had seen
him, too. My stomach fluttered at the thought of being
with Eli again. But I squashed it. I did not want him hurt,
which he would be if he remained in my company. Having almost died at the king's hand, I saw too clearly the
danger I brought him. We had no future together.

When the knock came, I did not have to wonder
who was at the door. I could sense him. "Come in."

The door opened and Eli burst through. I could not help but smile, my joy at seeing him nearly over-powering me. I longed to hold him, kiss him. I bowed my head before meeting his gaze.

"You are in good health?" he asked.

"I am healing quickly," I answered. "By the time the horses are ready, I should be like new."

He grinned. "You look beautiful."

"Thank you, sir." I curtsied.

When a knock sounded on the door, I collapsed onto a chair to appear frail. The young girl entered and in-formed us that our horses were ready. She handed Isa-bella two gowns and a satchel of dried meat and bread. I was not fully healed, but I would be soon enough.

Isabella and I drove the wagon while Eli rode alongside us. Though we looked like normal travel-ers, we carried our weapons within easy reach.

We did not expect to arrive at our next stop for a few more hours. It was going to be a long day and at the end of it, very likely, I would separate from Eli and his sister and never see them again. As much as I wanted to be with him, I would not allow myself to be the cause of his death or hers. I would rather be without him and know he was alive.

Seeing no point in pretending or hoping that Eli and I could be together, I ignored him at every oppor-tunity. He tried to touch my hand when we stopped to rest the horses and I shrank from him. When he spoke to me, I responded but averted my eyes. At first, he seemed confused. Since I had been so generous with my affections before, who could blame him? My chest squeezed with the knowledge that I had hurt him.

After several more failed attempts to engage me in conversation, his eyes tightened and his jaw set. I had angered him. But it was for the best.

CHAPTER THIRTEEN

WE HAD BEEN traveling for hours, only stopping for food. I wanted a few minutes to stretch my legs, maybe take a swim. My skin tingled, like it did not belong on me. Which, in a sense, it did not—I desperately needed to shift into a wolf. Soon.

I inhaled. Water was close by; I could smell it. I stretched higher on the wagon bench and scanned the area. A river glistened in the distance. It was small, and possibly shallow, but I did not care.

"Can we stop for water?" I asked loud enough for Eli to hear.

"We mustn't risk it," he threw over his shoulder. He immediately turned away from me and sped ahead on his horse.

I should not have been surprised at his reaction, since I had been so cold to him these last few hours. Still, I needed to get out of my human skin for a bit.

"It is not just my thirst I need to satisfy. Shifting now would be better, rather than waiting until we are surrounded by humans. Do you not agree?"

"Or you could skip it altogether." This time, he did

not even bother turning around.

"I am not like you, Eli," I shouted over the clop-pity-clop of the horses. "I cannot remain human in-definitely." I shook my head and brought a trembling hand to my forehead. "It has been too long already. I slept for an entire day instead of shifting."

Isabella sighed. "She is right, brother. We should make camp, at least for a little while."

Eli pulled to a stop and glared at me. "We must keep moving if we are to remain safe. Why not just shift into wolf now and follow us?"

"I fear I may get distracted and chase after prey instead of staying with the wagon." Why was he being so stubborn? He knew in our animal forms, we could not be relied upon to behave normally. "We are not necessarily of sound mind when we are not human."

His eyes followed my hand as I wiped a bead of sweat from my temple. His horse slowed when he pulled on the reins. "Go. We shall wait."

Leaping off the wagon, I changed into a wolf in midair. Once on solid ground, every muscle in my body strained as my paws beat against the ground toward the stream. As I neared the water, my lungs drew in the scent of damp earth.

From an embankment, I dove into the cool, shal-low liquid. It was deeper than it appeared from above and I rolled through the current, letting it soak my fur. I drifted to the bottom and floated along the ground as my muscles relaxed one by one.

Finally calm enough, I slowly made my way up.

When my ears broke the surface, I heard shouts and growls. My heart pounded in my chest as I raced to the wagon.

"Where is she?" a male voice growled.

"She is not with us," Eli replied, just before metal clanged against metal and swords clashed.

Four werewolves came into view and I moved carefully, so I would not make any noise. I sidled up against the back of the wagon and climbed up to see them better. One werewolf had a dagger at Isabella's neck. Eli stood still, sword ready as three others surrounded him. They may have outnumbered us, four against three, but I had the advantage of surprise — and being in my wolf form.

I crawled over the top of the wagon toward the three guards just beyond the horses, then leaped onto the back of the guard holding Isabella. My claws penetrated his skin and he released her to defend himself. As he growled and tried to shake me off, Isabella snatched the sword he had dropped. She shouted my name as she swung the blade in an arc and I jumped back. Blade met flesh and his head rolled on the ground.

Simultaneously triumphant and repulsed, I looked away and shivered.

Another guard rushed Isabella and she dodged him. Eli battled the remaining two guards. One held Eli while the other readied his sword. I attacked the one about to swing his blade and he tumbled to the ground with me.

I landed on top and my jaws clamped onto his

wrist. His free hand struck me over and over, but I stayed focused as my teeth ground through the flesh and bone. He screamed and struggled beneath me, but I held on until his hand dangled by only a tendon.

As I morphed to human and retrieved his sword, the one-handed guard changed into a wolf. But when he sprang toward me, snarling with bared teeth, I swung my sword. The blade sliced across his chest. The wolf yelped, his eyes wide, as he stumbled back. I silently thanked Eli and his sparring lessons.

But the wolf quickly recovered and he growled, circling me. I turned along with him, my sword ready. Behind me, I heard Isabella still struggling with the same werewolf. I had no idea if Eli was alive or dying, but I could not afford to take my eyes off my opponent. I would be of no use to either of them if I died.

As the wolf and I danced around each other, Eli came into my peripheral vision. Blood covered his shirt and he staggered when his sword sliced through the air. No doubt battling three wolves before I arrived had taken its toll on him. But he was alive. Unfortunately, so was his opponent.

The pawless wolf stopped for a moment, his eyes measuring me. Instead of charging him, I backed up and moved closer to Isabella and the werewolf she fought. Just a yard away, I spun, swung out my sword and cut off her opponent's head, then sprung away in time to miss being sliced in two by Eli's opponent—which gave Eli a moment to catch his breath.

Free now, Isabella bounded onto the wagon and

the pawless wolf jumped me from behind. My shoulder screamed in agony as we crashed against the ground. I reached for the dagger in my bodice, thankful it morphed with me. Just as I positioned the blade to sink into his chest, he collapsed on top of me.

"It is only a stab wound. It will heal." Isabella's shadow fell over me. "You had better cut off his head before he wakes."

I rolled the wolf off me in time to see Eli clawing at hands on his throat. Isabella wielded her sword with both hands and swiped the werewolf's shoulder. When he released Eli, she sliced through the air again and the werewolf's head dropped with a thud.

I shuddered again.

With trembling legs, I rose to stand in front of the werewolf Isabella had disabled moments before, the one I had rolled off me. He groaned. With all my force, I thrust the dagger across his throat and nudged the head away from the body.

Bile rose up from my stomach.

"Brother, can you hear me." Isabella patted his cheek.

"He is still in possession of his head. He will be fine. Eventually." I scooped him up and laid him in the back of the wagon. "I will ride the horse. You steer the wagon. If they were able to alert others when they found us, more of them are already on their way. We must make haste."

Isabella grabbed the reins and the wagon began to move. I mounted the horse and followed. A few minutes later, Eli stirred and I willed myself not to glance at him. He would be fine. He had no need for me to hover over him.

Unfortunately, *I* needed me to hover. Following my heart, I dug my heels into my horse's sides and she picked up her pace. As I came up alongside the wagon, I glanced over and met Eli's gaze.

"Feeling all right?" I asked.

"I have been better."

I nodded and averted my eyes. He was alive. That was all I needed to concern myself with.

"My dear sister, you are more formidable than I remember." He flashed her a wide smile when she turned around.

"Years of being trapped in a cage gave me reason to fight harder, dear brother. I will never let them lock me up again."

I envied their easy relationship and wished that one day I would share a love so deep that nothing could break the bond.

Hours later, the village came into view and we stopped to change our clothes. Eli had healed by then and sat upright in the wagon. Minutes later, we reached a port. We reined in our horses and I turned mine to face Eli and Isabella.

"Regardless of our destination, they will track us simply by finding out where the ships went. Do you have a plan?" I asked.

"Yes." Eli nodded. "But whether it is a good one or not, I cannot be sure."

CHAPTER FOURTEEN

TO SAVE TIME, we split up to inquire about the destination of every ship leaving port over the next few days. The wagon and horses would have only slowed us down and given the guards another way to track us, so we sold them to a local merchant for half what they were worth.

We took a room at the local inn before the next leg of our journey. Since I had already shifted to a wolf earlier that day and gotten that out of my system, I sat in the only chair and kept watch. Isabella and Eli slept, gathering their strength to get us to our next destination.

Eli lay sprawled out on one of the beds, his breathing rhythmic. I studied his peaceful face and my heart ached. I wanted to throw myself at his mercy and beg forgiveness for being so cold. But I could not. He and Isabella would live longer without me.

Once we reached our next stop, we would separate and would likely never see each other again. Tears welled in my eyes at the thought.

They had been sleeping for nearly three hours

when I heard a rustle outside the window. I stretched my senses beyond the wall but could not pick up on anything. Not with a barrier between us.

I sat perfectly still and stared at the drape-covered window. As I rose slowly, the candlelight flickered and shapes moved around the room. I leaned over and blew out the flame. Lanterns provided just enough light outside that I could see shadows move past the window.

The shadow could have been human, but it could just as easily have been a werewolf. The king's guards usually hunted and traveled in packs of four. If we saw one, I could assume there were three more nearby. Once again, we would be outnumbered.

Eli! Isabella! I shouted into their heads so only they would hear. If that was a guard outside, I did not want him alerted. *Wake up!*

They bolted upright, immediately on alert.

Someone is out there, I told them. We needed to be ready to run at any moment, so I grabbed the satchel of gold, along with the sword and scabbard, then stowed them around my waist. I found the bow and quiver and slung them over my shoulder, then made sure the dagger was in my bodice.

Isabella gathered what she wanted, then checked to make sure the drapes provided no openings. She remained there, sword ready in case someone crashed through the window. Eli crept toward the door, also armed with a sword. I stayed just behind Eli, ready to attack anyone who got past him.

A moment later, the door splintered and one of the king's guards burst into the room. Eli shifted into a giant bear and lunged at the intruder but another guard entered, then another and another. I leapt out from behind Eli and, with a swing of the sword, one guard's head dropped with a thud. The guard behind him dove for me, my back slamming against the hardwood floor. I struck out at him and his lip split open before he pinned my arms down.

A short blade flew past me and sank into the forehead of my attacker. He slumped forward on top of me. He would heal, but for now, he was incapacitated. I rolled him over and sprang to my feet. Two guards down. Two to go. One of them was punching Isabella in the face. She was fighting back, but a shape-shifter could never match a werewolf's strength. She was weakening.

Eli had shifted into a bear, his size making up for his opponent's greater strength. The guard gripped his sword as he struggled against Eli's jaws tightening around his neck. Though Eli appeared to be at an advantage, his bloody shirt told me he was wounded. I had a feeling Isabella needed my help more.

She lay trapped beneath a guard who was slamming his fist into her ribs. My stomach clenched at the idea of abandoning Eli, but I could not look him in the eye if I allowed his sister to die. I positioned my bow and plucked an arrow from the quiver and aimed. The arrow flew, sticking in the guard's back. He growled and turned. I raised my bow and directed another arrow at his face. I let my fingers straighten and the arrow sunk into his eye socket. Blood oozed down his cheek as he raced toward me.

In one fluid motion, I released an arrow into his neck. As I reached for another arrow, Isabella rose from the floor, and stumbled. I raised my bow, but was unable get another shot before he crashed into me, knocking me into the wall. The next instant, his head tumbled off his shoulders and Isabella came into view holding a bloody sword.

"Thank you," I told her, shrugging off the dead werewolf. I stepped around the body and followed Isabella's gaze.

Eli was staggering back as the blood-drenched guard stepped forward, blade thrusting toward Eli. I snagged an arrow, but Isabella was already swinging her sword. The next moment, the guard toppled to the floor. Eli shifted back into his human form and slid to the ground.

She knelt at her brother's side, though she moved with difficulty. "How badly are you hurt?"

He shook his head. "Nothing that will not heal soon enough. I just need a few minutes. You should take some time, too." He grinned up at her. "Still angry over all those hours I forced you to train with me?"

She returned his smile. "You were a tyrant. But had you not taught me how to fight, I would likely be dead."

I moved beside him, checking for injuries. He had plenty of cuts and scrapes, but I was relieved to find nothing so deep it would not be gone in a matter of moments. I grabbed a piece of dried meat from the satchel and shoved it at him. I retrieved another serving and handed it to Isabella. She had no outward signs of injury, but she had taken a beating.

As Eli chewed and swallowed, his eyes became more focused. I handed him more and a werewolf behind me stirred.

"I shall see to him." I left Isabella to care for Eli and grabbed my sword. I swung it hard as the werewolf pushed off the ground. Squeezing my eyes shut, I turned away as the blade met flesh. Though I saw nothing, my stomach churned at the crunch of bone and flesh.

"We must leave at once." Eli stood up, looking stronger by the second. "Isabella, are you well enough?"

"I fear I have no other choice. We may have to make extra stops to rest until we are both fully recovered." She switched to me. "Are you ready?"

In just moments, we would be gone. Now that we had slain our enemy—this round—we were closer to freedom. And I was closer to losing him forever.

I reminded myself that he had never been mine to keep. Still, I tried to imagine my life without Eli and the harder I tried, the more my head spun. I needed to make sure I had all my things, but I could not move, as though my feet had grown roots.

"Hannah, are you all right?" Isabella asked as she bustled about the room, collecting what we would need for the next leg of our journey.

"I do not know," I mumbled, unable to pick up my feet. We had defeated our enemies, but for what? Either way, I could not be with the man I loved. What was the point in fighting? Suddenly, I was exhausted and could not bear the thought of going on alone.

"I think she is in shock," Isabella whispered.

Energy swirled around me and I assumed Eli and Isabella were speaking telepathically. About me, I was sure. They probably thought I had lost my mind since I had suddenly gone mute. I did not care. My throat swelled with the need to release a flood of tears. But I would not allow myself to do that in front of Eli. He needed to be able to leave me free and clear with no regrets.

"I am replacing your sword," Isabella said as the blade slid into the scabbard. "It has been a long day and you fought well. Eli and I will take care of everything from here."

I nodded, my eyes blurring. I was about to lift my foot when I felt a slight tug on the strap of my quiver and heard a *plunk* as an arrow slid inside. The satchel at my shoulder jingled while Isabella checked the contents. Then she moved away, taking her sweet, woodsy scent with her. I stood there frozen as a breeze from the window moved a lock of my hair.

"Eli, wait," Isabella said. "I prepared a bag earlier with supplies we might need." Rope brushed my hair as she hung the bag around my neck.

"Under normal circumstances, I might commend you for your quick thinking," he said. "But we must travel light."

"A tin cup for water, some spices I talked the cook out of this morning and a thin blanket," she explained as she looped yet another bag around my neck.

"Fine. We need to move." Eli picked me up, jumped out the window and gingerly set my feet on the ground, his hands wrapped around my arm.

Isabella followed and sidled up to me, taking my other arm in her hands. The next instant, their hands became giant claws which dragged me into the air.

† † †

My eyelids fluttered open to see the sun glowing behind a puffy white cloud. Trees swayed around me and a soft wind whispered against my skin.

"Good morning." Isabella leaned over me and brought a piece of dried meat to my mouth. "We were concerned about you."

As I chewed, guilt washed over me for making them worry. Physically, nothing was wrong. Isabella was wasting her time trying to nurse me back to health — my problem was something else entirely.

Where was Eli? Any time now, we would say goodbye and he would be lost to me forever.

After I swallowed a few bites, she held a tin cup against my lips. I gulped until the cup was empty, then propped myself up on my elbows.

Isabella beamed. "You look much better."

"It was not anything serious," I replied. "Just exhausted."

"You may rest as long as you wish." She took the cup back and set it aside.

"How far did we fly?" I asked.

Soon after we had taken flight from the inn, I welcomed the oblivion of unconsciousness. All I had known at the time was that we were flying north since the guards would expect us to travel by ship—which were all traveling south. Eli and Isabella had stopped to rest, but I had fallen asleep again as soon as we were once again in the air.

"We passed Scotland and landed on one of the unpopulated islands. Even if by some miracle the guards figure out which direction we went, it could take weeks or months before they find this island. By then, we will have moved on." Isabella held out another piece of dried meat. "We will be quite safe here for some time, I assure you."

I took the meat and fell back against the makeshift pillow, relief flooding me. "When you leave, would you take me to Norway? I think I should like to go to Moscow by way of Finland."

"That is a very long way to fly. We will have to make many stops." She shook her head, and then a mischievous smile curved her lips. "How fortunate for you we are going there anyway."

My stomach fluttered at the sound of shoes crunching against sand and rock. Not wanting Eli to catch me in bed, I threw off the thin blanket and rose.

I met Eli's hard gaze and my chest squeezed. He must dislike me now for treating him so coldly. But it was just as well. Soon, werewolves all over would hear about our escape and the king would offer a reward. Any guards who spotted us—two shape-shifters with a werewolf—would immediately attempt to kill us and bring our heads to the king. The sooner we separated, the safer we would be.

Isabella cleared her throat. "I feel the need for a swim. I shall return in a while." She backed away and disappeared into the trees.

I dropped my gaze to his feet. "How soon shall we leave?"

"Isabella and I must rest for the night. We can leave at first light."

I nodded, angling myself away so I would not have to meet his gaze. "And once we arrive at our destination, it will no longer be necessary to travel together."

CHAPTER FIFTEEN

"NO. IT WAS of great benefit to stay together and necessary in order to gain freedom these past few days." Eli waited a beat and stepped closer.

I only had to reach out to touch him, press my mouth to his warm skin. "And now we no longer need each other," I whispered.

He inched closer until I could feel his warm breath against my ear. "I may not *need* you to survive, but I *want* you."

"You want me?" I blinked, shaking my head. Simply wanting was not enough. Even if Eli's feelings were stronger, he could not know what he was saying. "With me comes danger. Apart, we will both live longer."

"This is all true. And I must admit that your recent indifference toward me..." His breath whooshed out as he shook his head. "I felt betrayed. But on the way here to the island, I had little else to do but think." He leaned in until his breath tickled my cheek. "You told me you loved me and I cannot believe deception is in your nature. Therefore, I must assume fear is driving you to say such things."

Tears pooled in my eyes as I took a step back. "Being together and risking our lives will be the stupidest thing we could possibly do."

His eyes lit up as if I had just confirmed his assumptions. "I would choose a shorter life with you than a long, miserable life without you."

"You would risk your life to be with me, a werewolf, your natural enemy?"

"I would risk everything for the one I love." He closed the distance and reached up to slide his fingers behind my neck, pressing his forehead to mine. "Fighting for our own happiness could never be wrong. If we do not stand up for what is right, I see no point in living. Is that not why you left the king?"

I sucked in a shaky breath. "We will always be looking over our shoulder."

"We will be doing that regardless. By now, the king has sketches distributed and everyone is looking for a blond shifter and a raven-haired werewolf. They will *always* search for us whether we are together or not." Eli's lips curved up and he brushed them against my cheek. A tingle spread over my skin. "If I am destined to be hunted regardless, I must have you with me."

My fist clamped onto the fabric of his shirt as I drank in his earthy sweet scent. Eli was right. Either way, we would spend the rest of our lives looking over our shoulders. If we were to separate, what would happen when the next four werewolves found us? Surely, we were safer together where we could protect each other. And if I died, I wanted Eli's scent to be the last thing I breathed. I would rather have weeks with Eli than eternity without him.

"Then we will run together, because I cannot imagine my life without you." I started to slide my hand around his neck when he grasped it.

He bent, pressed his lips to the back of my hand and met my gaze. "You will always be my queen, for as long as you will have me."

That would be forever. And I did not care how many werewolves hunted us. I had no intention of being cheated out of even one second of my time with Eli. I smiled up at him. "Always."

He tucked a strand of hair behind my ear and I held my breath as he slowly leaned in. His lips softly brushed against mine and I knew I would always yield, always do whatever I needed so we would survive.

This was the beginning of our forever together.

THE END

To read the exciting epilogue that launches the Shapes of Autumn series, please visit
VERONICABLADE*.com*
and sign up for Veronica's newsletter.
Once you're subscribed, we will send you a welcome email, asking if you'd like the epilogue pdf.
Simply reply with a request
& we'll get it out to you shortly.

Thank you so much for reading and we hope you enjoyed Hannah and Eli's story.
If you enjoyed this book, please recommend it to friends, reader's groups and discussion boards or tell others how much you enjoyed it by reviewing it on Amazon, GoodReads or your own site. Thank you and happy reading!

† † †

BOOKS IN THE SHAPES OF AUTUMN SERIES:

Thrown to the Wolves: The Legend of Hannah & Eli
(Shapes of Autumn, prequel)

My Wolf's Bane (Shapes of Autumn, book one)

Wolves at the Door (Shapes of Autumn, book two)

Thown to the Wolves (Shapes of Autumn, book two)

Dead Wolf Walking (Shapes of Autumn, book three)

The Dark Wolf (Shapes of Autumn, book four)

Lord of the Wolves (Shapes of Autumn, book five)

ACKNOWLEDGMENTS

MY HAT GOES off to anyone who writes historical. Folks, this was not easy! Thankfully, I had my very talented writer pals PR Mason, Laura Sheehan and Felice Fox to help. And special assistance from the amazing Robin Haseltine—love her! As always, big hugs to Susan Hatler for everything she does.

I'm also grateful to everyone who read the earlier versions of Thrown to the Wolves, like Megan Durrence and Shelby Ray—and the list goes on. Thank you all so much!!

A big, fat thanks to Sara E who is ALWAYS there for me and many others whose enthusiasm for my stories keeps me believing in my writing. And a very special hell-yeah to Rose Nomura for her gorgeous cover design!

Last, but not least, a big kiss to my wonderful hubs who puts up with being ignored for hours on end, so I can follow my dream. Baby, I'm so glad you're mine!

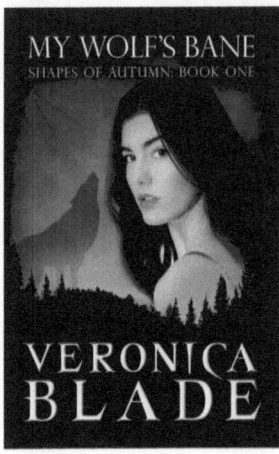

More Titles by Veronica Blade

A newbie witch enlists help from the scrumptious school bad-boy to make her life and death choice between two battling covens.

A Cinderella who spends her nights as a wolf. A prince with a taste for blood.

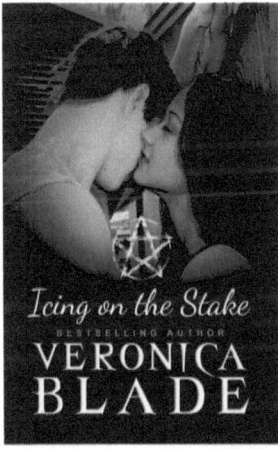

Sofia lays her hard-won anonymity on the line by saving the most popular boy in school. Worse, she's been exposed to the vampire hunters who attacked him.

The witch queen must make the impossible choice between abandoning the throne and her people, or spending eternity with the man she loves.

More Titles by Veronica Blade

Should a woman who's unable to forget her first love give "happily ever after" one more try?

When good-girl Maddie switches places with her famous bad-girl twin Jackie, she has some pretty high stilettos to fill.

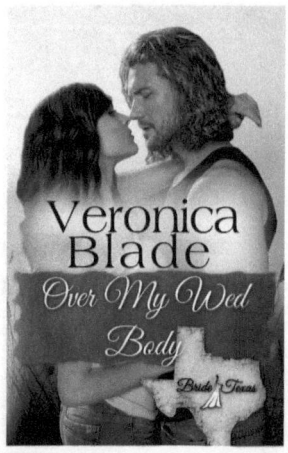

When Hunter realizes he botched the annulment of his marriage to his longtime friend, he must decide if she and their marriage are worth fighting for.

A micro trilogy including Single-Handed, Singled Out (book two) & Single-minded (book three).

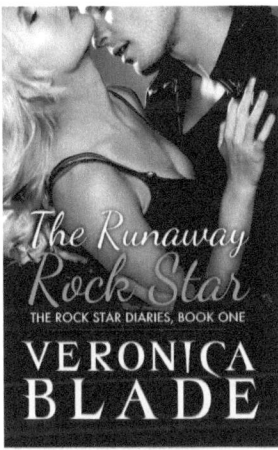
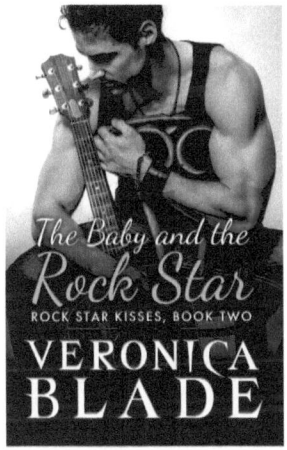
† † †

For updates on releases, please visit
www.VERONICABLADE.com

ABOUT VERONICA BLADE

VERONICA BLADE LIVES near Carson City, Nevada with her husband and furbabies but also spends a lot of time in southern California. She writes sweet romances to live vicariously through her characters. Except her heroes and heroines lead far more interesting lives—and they are always way hotter.

)

You can visit Veronica Blade on Facebook, check out her website at VeronicaBlade.com or follow her on Twitter @VeronicaBlade. You can even e-mail her at veronica@ veronicablade.com. She loves hearing from readers!

www.ingramcontent.com/pod-product-compliance
Lightning Source LLC
Chambersburg PA
CBHW030622130626
46552CB00002B/673